INCIDENT AT
COPPER CREEK

INCIDENT AT COPPER CREEK

•

Michael Senuta

AVALON BOOKS
NEW YORK

PRINTED IN THE UNITED STATES OF AMERICA
ON ACID-FREE PAPER
BY HADDON CRAFTSMEN, BLOOMSBURG, PENNSYLVANIA

To my parents, William and Cathyrnne

Chapter One

T race Hawthorne had been standing in the alleyway next to the hotel for a long time. He was far from the nearest lamppost, in a place where the shadows blanketed him, enabling him to go unnoticed while he observed those few townsmen who were still up and about at this late hour.

If one could penetrate the darkness, one would see a broad-shouldered man, six foot, two inches tall. Yet there was a lean look to him that belied his two hundred and twenty pounds. Countless days on the range had taken their toll on his otherwise handsome face, for tiny lines had formed around his dark eyes, and skin the color of a walnut bore testimony to his lifelong relationship with a relentless sun.

When the last footfalls had died away and the street was left to the crickets and moonlight, he moved onto the boardwalk and made for the hotel entrance. For a big man, he was remarkably light on his feet. There was an economy to his movements, a certitude about his actions. On his hip was a pearl-handled Colt .45, encased in black leather, tied down around his thigh. On his vest was a badge that read: U.S. Marshal.

The hotel lobby was empty, the desk clerk having long since retired for the evening. Thickly padded armchairs, potted ferns, and shiny mahogany tables formed the decor. An understated but nonetheless impressive chandelier cast a gentle glow throughout the room. Hawthorne climbed the stairs to the second floor. They were broad stairs, thickly carpeted with a pattern of tiny interlocking squares that suited the quiet elegance of the establishment. The corridor that accessed the rooms on the second floor was also wide. The ceiling was high. The wallpaper hinted its message through cordial pastels; gilded gaslights flickered softly—the combination of which left one in an atmosphere soothing to the eye.

Two bulky men wearing derbies and suits stood midway down the corridor, positioned on either side of one of the doors. They stiffened a bit when Hawthorne approached, but upon recognizing him, they nodded and shifted their stances slightly. Without turning, one of them gently tapped his knuckles on the door behind him. There was a short pause, followed by a muffled response from within. The man opened the door and stepped aside. Hawthorne entered, closing the door after him.

The room was dim, lit only by a single lamp somewhere off to Hawthorne's left. After his eyes acclimated to the light, Hawthorne saw a settee, a large round table littered with papers, a bureau, and a side table with a pitcher and basin. A delicate breeze barely moved the curtains on the only window in the room. Facing the window was a high backed chair. The strong aroma of cigar smoke filled the air.

"Good evening, Marshal," a voice barely above a whisper announced.

Hawthorne saw no one, but he watched as the chair swivelled slowly and a man rose from it and walked toward him. The man was barely five-feet-five, and Hawthorne towered over him. He was about sixty-five, with gray hair, a neatly trimmed gray mustache, and a gaunt face. His shoulders were hunched, and his entire body seemed to move painfully with each step he took. He wore a dark suit with a gold chain that dangled from his vest pocket.

"Governor," Hawthorne replied as he removed his Stetson.

For a long moment the governor said nothing. He merely puffed on his cigar as he regarded Hawthorne through eyes that seemed to be nothing more than narrow slits carved in his emaciated face. "I trust that you were not observed coming here?" he finally asked.

"No, sir."

The governor nodded slightly, yet his eyes did not leave Hawthorne's face. "Are you adequately equipped?"

"I am."

"Very well." He strolled over to the table and waved his cigar over the papers that lay scattered before him.

"It's hard to conceive that the entire history of a man's life can be contained on a few pieces of paper . . . yet here it is . . . the life of one Maximilian McCargo. An appropriate name, don't you think, for the individual in question? I wonder if he ever entertained any ideas of actually attaining emperor status?"

Hawthorne's thoughts ran wild as he considered the name and the documents before him.

"It's the history of one of the most hideous men who ever lived. A man who led a life of treachery, greed, deceit, and violence. But now, with everything in place, with your help, and the Almighty's guidance, we may finally see an end to Maximilian McCargo and his reign of terror." As the governor spoke, he opened a drawer and extracted a folded piece of paper, which he handed to Hawthorne.

Hawthorne unfolded it, and read the words carefully.

His eyes still focused on Hawthorne, the governor asked, "Is everything understood?"

"Yes, sir," Hawthorne replied.

The governor extended his hand, and Hawthorne returned the paper. Puffing on his cigar, the governor strolled over to the table and dropped the paper into an ashtray. He then ignited it with his cigar. A tiny flame suddenly flared into a bright light, but only for a moment, as it died down, leaving only a small mound of ashes.

Hawthorne watched as the governor turned away, stepped to the window, and peered around the curtains. With his back to Hawthorne, he said, "It's a warm night. I remember nights like this when I was a boy back in Missouri. Sometimes I wish I would have stayed there—on the river—and been a boy forever."

He turned slowly, breaking from his reverie, and faced Hawthorne. "I can't begin to impress upon you the significance of this mission. A great many threads are now in place, but the most important thread of all is entrusted to you. Adam Malverne is our star witness. Unless you can deliver him on the prescribed day and time, months of work will go for naught. Many crimes will go unavenged. Many more may be committed unless McCargo is stopped."

He walked across the room and stopped just inches away from Hawthorne, staring hard at his face, scrutinizing him with his narrow eyes. "You know how far McCargo's power extends. He has bought more people than you or I could imagine. Those he can't buy he kills . . . and he has the guns to do it. He has no choice now but to kill because his back is against the wall. If we can prove our case, he'll hang. He has killed most of those who would dare testify against him. The others are too afraid, and I can't say I blame them. Malverne is our main hope. As McCargo's bookkeeper, he knows names, dates, places . . . he knows where the bodies are buried. With his testimony, we can get a conviction. Without him, in spite of all the other evidence we have amassed, the attorney general believes we have no better chance than one in ten."

"I understand."

"When will you leave?"

"Tonight. There's a full moon. I'd like to be far from town by daybreak."

The governor nodded. "I want you to know that there have been two attempts on Malverne's life since we've taken him into protective custody. I've lost one man, and another is in the hospital. Chances are he'll never walk again. There are few people I trust. You're one of them. You know this territory like the back of your hand, and you're one of the best there is with that," the governor said, pointing at the Colt holstered on Hawthorne's hip, "yet it's long odds I'm giving you. Still, if *you* can't get him there, no one can."

"I'll get him there . . . or die trying," Hawthorne stated.

"I know the reasons that drive you, son. Don't let them cloud your judgment. Remember that badge that you carry. Don't ever let anything get in its way."

Hawthorne considered the advice soberly and nodded.

The governor blew a few puffs of smoke into the air and then removed his cigar. He contemplated it as he held it between his fingers. "The doctors tell me I don't have much longer. They tell me these are bad for me." He chuckled. "I smoke them anyway. Why shouldn't I? Except for an occasional glass of bourbon, they're my only pleasure now. I only hope I live long enough to take pleasure in seeing McCargo hang. If I can witness that, it will be the crowning achievement of my career."

He moved to the table and snuffed out the cigar in the ashtray. Slowly, he turned toward Hawthorne and threw a stare that would have branded the hide of a bull. "Keep Malverne alive, Marshal, and get him to that courtroom. Get him there at all costs."

Hawthorne left the hotel, made a quiet and circuitous walk through a series of alleys to a stable, where he secured two saddled horses—a chestnut and a bay—and a pack mule. He checked his Winchester, shells, canteens, and supplies. He then led the animals from their stalls, out of the stable, to a small clearing in a grove of aspens a quarter of a mile west of town. Here, he waited.

It was a pleasant evening. An owl hooted somewhere off in the distance, and the leaves of the aspens trembled in the warm breeze. Otherwise, there was a blanket of silence over the land. Hawthorne surveyed the town through the trees. An occasional lamppost, coupled with the light of the moon, helped outline the sizes and shapes of the buildings.

Twenty minutes later, a small circle of men appeared through the darkness. Their soft tread was barely audible even as they neared the clearing. Hawthorne recognized two of the men as having stood guard in the hotel corridor. One carried a shotgun; the other held a Winchester. The others were similarly armed. They stopped some fifteen feet from where Hawthorne stood. They were vigilant, alert. For a moment, no one moved, and then one element separated itself from the group and continued on a straight line through the clearing to Hawthorne. As if on cue, the others turned without a word and disappeared into the night.

Hawthorne assessed the man who stood before him. He was about thirty-five, with a slight build. He carried his left arm in a sling. He wore trail clothes but looked awkward in them. He wore no weapon. His face was somber, an almost defeated expression etched upon it. He stared at Hawthorne as though he were looking through him. Hawthorne pointed to one of the horses, and the man climbed into the saddle. They left the clearing, riding through the aspens without exchanging a word.

Dawn seemed to find the forest in its own good time, chasing the night, spreading its notions on a new day. Bands of clouds became visible, painting the heavens with their signatures in red and pink.

Neither man had spoken since the journey had begun, but that was not unusual on the trail, where a traveler had to be aware of his surroundings, his outfit, and his own limitations. Although Malverne did not admit to it, he was tired. Hawthorne could see that his face was drawn and his shoulders were bowed. He decided to make camp, for they could both use the rest.

Hawthorne selected a spot he knew well—a clearing where a small stream ran lazily through a stretch of ponderosa pines. He removed the saddles and blankets from the horses and unloaded the pack from the mule. He watered the animals and then hobbled them. The grass was good and plentiful. He had barely finished

Malverne laughed in disgust. "You don't understand. Mr. McCargo doesn't do anything. He lives in a big ranch house on a big spread . . . when he isn't celebrating his newest acquisitions over oysters and champagne in the finest suite of the finest hotel. He has others do things for him."

"Such as Mace Gorman?" Hawthorne asked, his eyes leveled on the rim of his cup.

"Yes, such as Mace Gorman," Malverne returned, with a surprised voice at the mention of the name. "Mace Gorman is his . . . lieutenant. He does anything and everything for Mr. McCargo."

"Including murder?"

"Yes, including murder. What's more, he enjoys it. Gorman alone is a handful, but he has a dozen other top guns at his disposal."

"You mean like Brill Cotton and Avery Truman?"

Malverne bristled at the names. He eyed Hawthorne narrowly. "You know about them, do you?"

"I do."

"The governor told me that you were a lawman. That I can see by your badge. He also said your name wasn't important. Just who are you?"

Hawthorne set his cup on a rock. "The governor was right. My name isn't important."

"Even so, I'd like to know. Since my life is on the line as well as yours, I figure I've got a claim to know who rides with me."

Hawthorne considered Malverne's words and decided that he had a point. "My name is Hawthorne."

before Malverne had fallen asleep. He lay sprawled awkwardly on the ground, his head resting on his saddle. Hawthorne, too, stretched out, his Winchester within reach, his hand near his Colt.

Four hours later, Hawthorne awoke to the hammering of a woodpecker and the rhythmic trickling of the stream. Refreshed and renewed, his eyes gradually focused on the sun's rays as they filtered through the pine needles of the outstretched limbs above. It was peaceful here, he thought, far from the towns and settlements where men too often existed by cheating and robbing and killing one another.

He allowed himself a moment to reflect on his past. He had never given much thought to his future, for he was driven primarily by one goal. In all the years he had been a lawman, his profession had consumed him, having left him with little time for those things in life most men enjoyed, particularly during the last year when he had existed exclusively within the governor's personal orbit. He drank very little. Of the few women with whom he had been closely linked, he knew none he would consider living with on a permanent basis. He was, he concluded upon closer self-examination, a one-dimensional man. Yet, good or bad, right or wrong, it was what he was, and more than likely, it was what he would always be.

His thoughts ran randomly along these lines for several minutes before his concentration returned to the situation at hand and his responsibilities. Malverne was still asleep, stretched out in virtually the same position he had assumed when he had first lain down.

Hawthorne scanned the camp and the run of pines. Satisfied that everything was as it should be, he rose slowly to his feet, tried his legs, and strolled over to the stream, where he washed and drank.

Fifteen minutes later, he had a cheerful fire going, coffee brewing, and bacon sizzling. He ate heartily while Malverne slept, giving the man as much rest as possible. When he had completed his second cup, he walked over to Malverne and nudged his shoulder. Malverne stirred, turned stiffly, and then massaged the arm that he carried in a sling. Grudgingly, he opened his eyes and sat up. Hawthorne set coffee and a plate in front of him and returned to the pot and poured himself a third cup.

"Thanks," Malverne said, picking up the cup and blowing on the strong, hot brew. "How long did I sleep?"

"About four hours."

Malverne groaned.

"I'd like to get started as soon as possible. We've got quite a bit of ground to cover."

"Really? I thought we rode halfway across the state last night."

"Hardly."

Malverne picked up the plate and balanced it on his lap. Favoring his left hand, he began cutting the bacon into neat sections about one inch square. These he ate methodically, dabbing his bread occasionally, and sipping from his cup at regular intervals. When he finished, he nodded appreciatively.

"More coffee?"

"No, thanks."

"I know my coffee's bad, but one cup won't keep you going. We may not eat again for a long time."

"The coffee's fine. You'd only be wasting it on me."

"How's that?"

"Because there's no way that you're going to get me to Grand City alive. Mr. McCargo won't let you."

"We'll see."

Malverne carelessly tossed the remains of his coffee onto the ground. "I don't know what plans you and the governor have worked out, but I can tell you right now that this is all a waste of time. It was just pure luck that I escaped from being killed back in Porterville. By all accounts, I should be six feet under right now."

"Is that how you got that?" Hawthorne asked, indicating the sling on Malverne's arm.

"That's right. There was an ambush set up—on the main street of town in broad daylight. Some of M McCargo's hired guns. One of the governor's m stepped in front of me. He took most of the load fr a shotgun. A stray ball struck me in the arm. It pr ably should've been the other way around," Malv said, staring at the ground at his feet.

"McCargo has to be stopped."

"Mr. McCargo is too powerful to be stopped. he can't buy, he runs off. Those with a little ba that he can't run off, he kills."

"McCargo is being held in a cell right now bond."

Malverne's eyes widened. "Trace Hawthorne out of Spencer?"

"Formerly."

"I remember an incident just over two years ago. Mr. McCargo was trying to obtain a piece of property that would have given him access to a railhead near your neck of the woods. There was a family of squatters there who had title to the land."

Hawthorne nodded. "The Graingers."

"That's the name. Mr. McCargo applied pressure, but they wouldn't give up their claim."

"So he tried to burn them out. A twelve-year-old girl still carries scars from that fire."

Malverne pursed his lips. "Mr. McCargo used two of his best gunmen on that job—the Blanton brothers."

"They were handy."

"Word was that you shot it out with them. They never returned."

"McCargo should've sent better men."

"He never forgot that incident. It was one of the few times that he didn't get what he wanted. He never forgot your name either. He remembers things like that." Malverne passed his hand across his chin pensively. "There were other occasions . . . when Mr. McCargo was never certain, but your name kept cropping up. You seemed to interfere with his plans in subtle ways . . . inconveniencing him, delaying him. He kept his distance, partly because his operation was too big to worry about such minor details, and partly because you were federal. He didn't want to buy that kind of trouble, but now . . . he has no choice. From this moment on, you're as big a target as I am."

"I've been a target before."

"Mr. McCargo will stop at nothing to prevent me from testifying."

"In that case, Mr. McCargo and I have something in common because I'll stop at nothing to ensure that you do testify."

"I know your reputation. You're a gunfighter—maybe the best—but as I've told you, you're hopelessly outmanned and outgunned. The men that Mr. McCargo employs are bought and paid for—parcel and package. He buys men the way a lady buys hats."

"That's my worry."

"That's a tall order, Marshal, even for a man of your abilities."

Hawthorne emptied his cup and climbed to his feet. "Finish your meal. It's time to break camp."

The day's travel was productive but uneventful. They passed through forests of pines and firs, rode through fields of wildflowers that teemed with butterflies and bees, and forded a river in which the crystal, clear water shimmered like silver in the afternoon sun. Elk were plentiful, and once they spotted a large black bear lumbering across a field of goldenrods, oblivious to their presence. They stopped half an hour before the sun lost its strength and as long shadows draped the land. Hawthorne made camp and started supper.

Malverne ate sparingly, picking erratically at his food and staring vacantly into the flames of the campfire. Hawthorne respected his silence and sat on the opposite side. He as well was occupied with his own concerns. He had seen tracks earlier in the day—two shod mounts bearing riders, with two unshod riderless horses in tow. The tracks were fresh, not more than two or three hours old. They might have been Shoshones, but this far south, he somehow doubted it. It was probably nothing more than some itinerant travelers; still, Hawthorne wondered. In the morning he would veer further south, favoring a different trail in order to minimize any contact with strangers. On this night he would keep the horses closer to the fire, and he would sleep light.

Chapter Two

Max McCargo leaned casually against the wall, admiring the rolled tobacco leaves that he turned over in his hand. The thin worm of smoke rising from the exclusive blend of his cigar left a pleasant aroma in his cell, compensating somewhat for the bleak walls, lumpy mattress, and dusty floor. He was a big man, six-foot-four, barrel-chested, with a sizeable paunch around his middle. He wore an expensive black suit, a silk vest, and a pair of the finest leather boots shined to perfection. His dark, curly hair was thinning; his mustache was precisely trimmed.

The sound of a key turning in a lock aroused his attention, and he turned to see one of the town deputies opening the outer door. The deputy stepped aside and admitted a dapper-looking man of about fifty, wearing a brown suit. Waiting for the door to close behind him, the man stepped over to the cell and smiled.

"Good morning, Mr. McCargo. Are you comfortable? Can I get you anything? More cigars?"

"Skip the pleasantries, Blake, and get down to business. You're my lawyer, not my servant," McCargo said.

Blake stiffened. His smile dissolved, and he stood in front of the cell as if he were offering a plea in court. "Everything is ready for trial. I've been preparing—"

"Forget the speech. We both know that Malverne can destroy me if he testifies. I want him to disappear before he gets within fifty miles of Grand City. Now, I know our first two attempts have failed. What's the latest as to his whereabouts?"

"We know that he met with the governor yesterday. He's being moved south under heavy escort, and we believe he'll be placed on the train at Porterville."

McCargo took a long drag on his cigar and released a thick plume of blue smoke that curled around the bars and drifted upward. His eyes followed the progress of a beetle as it crawled across the floorboards at his feet. "I don't think so."

"How's that?"

"I don't think the governor will place Malverne aboard a train."

"But, Mr. McCargo, he can maintain the highest possible security on a train. It seems to me—"

"No. The governor knows that if he had a hundred

armed men on a train, he wouldn't be able to stop us from destroying the train itself. There are a thousand secluded places between Porterville and Grand City where the track could be blown, the train derailed, and his precious witness killed. No, it has to be something more subtle than that. The governor has wanted me for too long. He won't make it that easy for me to remove Malverne and destroy his case."

"But our informant in the governor's pay assured us that—"

"The informant is wrong. Either he's gotten simple-minded, or they're onto him."

"But the escort?"

McCargo brushed some ashes off his vest as he pondered the situation. "Have some of our men follow the escort anyway. If the opportunity presents itself, they'll know what to do. But don't concentrate all our manpower on the escort. I'm guessing it's a blind. I want men at every town between the governor and Grand City. If we don't have enough men, hire more. Hire whatever it takes. Just get Malverne before he points the finger at me. Double the bounty on his head."

"Yes, sir, if that's the way you want it."

"That's exactly the way I want it, Blake. It's my way and no other."

Blake nodded.

"Now, where's Myra? She hasn't come by to see me in two days."

"Well, I thought, sir, in an effort to keep up appearances, that it would be more prudent for your image if Miss Fontaine not be seen with you. I mean, considering your wife's health and all."

"My wife's health is my concern and no one else's. Is that clear, Blake?"

Blake flinched.

"And when I say I want to see Myra, I want to see her. Escort her across the street yourself if it makes you feel any better. Maybe that way it will at least appear that there's some legal reason behind her visit."

"Mr. McCargo, I really don't think that would be—"

McCargo blew smoke through the bars into Blake's face. "Hadn't you'd better get moving? You've got some telegrams to send," McCargo said tersely.

Blake closed his eyelids as he stifled a cough. Awkwardly, he turned and made his way to the door.

McCargo sneered disdainfully, turned, tossed his cigar stub through the bars of the window, and sat down on the bunk. He pulled another cigar from the breast pocket of his coat, bit off the tip, and struck a match with his thumbnail. Soon the cell was filled with smoke, and he leaned back against the wall, cradling his head in his hand, and contemplated his situation.

He had taken a lifetime to build his empire, to attain his status. Cattle, mining, land development . . . he had his hand in everything that could turn a profit and serve to make him more powerful than the next man. Money and power. He never really considered which one was more important to him. He always assumed the two went hand in hand—and in his case, they did. A one-time self-appraisal of his position proved him to be one of the five wealthiest men in the state; in terms of influence and dominion, he reckoned himself to be second, certainly no less than third.

He held sway over every man he knew. He had a simple formula for dominance. Those he could not suborn or frighten, he removed. It had worked well for him these many years, but now his empire—his very freedom, perhaps his life—hung in the balance because of the potential testimony of a small, insignificant man he had hardly given any consideration to other than as a bookkeeper who now knew too much— more than enough to bring down the great Maximilian McCargo.

He would, no doubt, eliminate this man, and he would remember those whose efforts put him in this filthy cell. He would retaliate successfully against them in his own way, in his own time. He would break them in the same way he had broken so many others. They were all afraid of him—the sheriff, the deputies, the court authorities. He could see it in their eyes. Perhaps even the governor himself feared Max McCargo. He would crush them, and all the others would know it and remember it, and they would fear him for it.

McCargo leaned forward, stared at the beetle that had made its slow trek across the floor of the cell to within inches of his feet. He picked up his foot and stamped down hard on the insect, grinding it under the heel of his boot until there was nothing more of it than a liquid mess with his cigar ash on the cell floor.

* * *

Charles Blake left the jailhouse, walked down the boardwalk for a time, and then made his way into the street, where he sidestepped a buckboard before crossing to a large block of buildings that contained his office. He entered a small foyer before passing through an outer office where he was greeted by Mrs. Harker, an elderly widow who served as his secretary. She looked at him over her pince-nez, handed him some mail, and returned to the typewriter on her desk.

Blake entered his office, a spacious room lined with bookshelves containing law books. A leather settee, a pair of wing chairs, and a side table covered with crystal decanters and tumblers formed the general decor. In one corner was a highly burnished oak desk. On it were a lamp with a green shade, some documents, and a letter opener.

Blake hung his hat on a tree hook, tossed the mail Mrs. Harker had given him onto the desk, and moved directly to the side table. He half-filled a tumbler with whiskey and then sat down heavily on one of the chairs. He noticed that his hand was shaking as he raised the tumbler to his lips. With both hands he steadied the tumbler and drained it. He knew it was too early in the day to be drinking hard liquor. He had been doing it more and more lately. He had also been shaking more, for his nerves were shot. He placed the tumbler on the side table and pressed his fingers to his eyes. He was tired, but it was not the kind of fatigue that came with a hard day's work or even a week's labor. It was a grinding, monotonous fatigue that, coupled with fear, cut into a man, eroding his fiber, his very being, until it made him feel edgy and alone; until it left him questioning his ability in himself.

Blake understood his problem perfectly. Although once a highly principled counselor at law, a master in the courtroom, he was no longer certain of himself. His association with McCargo had done that to him. He had allowed himself to be subjugated to the wants and needs of another. Oh, he had benefited financially by riding the wave of McCargo's machine, but he had also allowed himself to be manipulated by it, the end result being that he had lost his individuality. His principles were shaken; his backbone was whiskey with a water chaser.

Secretly, he saluted Adam Malverne for what he was attempting to do. He only regretted that he had not been the one to stand up and act like a man instead of hiding among his law books and taking the abuse that Max McCargo dished out in massive and regular doses.

Shakily, Blake stood, gathered himself, and stepped to his desk. He sat down and waited for his hand to steady itself. Then, he selected several clean sheets of paper, thought for a moment, and began to script a series of coded messages. It took him fifteen minutes. When he was done, he collected his hat and made for the telegraph office.

A long-legged chanteuse, Myra Fontaine was the star attraction at the Cavanagh House—Grand City's major entertainment center. Actually, it was a saloon and gambling establishment, but it ran two shows at eight and ten every night but Sunday, featuring acts ranging from opera to Shakespeare to bawdy song-and-dance routines. Myra was currently enjoying celebrity status. She was quite popular among the citizens of Grand City—particularly the men—and, in fact, was quite talented in her own right. She was a trained singer with better-than-average range, had a flair for comedy, and was probably the most gorgeous woman ever to hit town.

Blake stood in front of the Cavanagh House for a long moment, admiring a life-sized poster that advertised Myra's performances and showed off her physical attributes. He turned down the alley, entered the establishment through a side door, walked up a flight of stairs, and found himself standing outside Myra's private dressing room and bath. He removed his hat, ran his fingers through his hair, and adjusted his tie. He knocked softly. "Come in," he heard, and passed into Myra's personal domain.

It was a room glorious enough for any hotel but particularly splendid for Grand City: decorative wallpaper, gilded sconces, plush carpeting, and a massive bed with an elaborately carved canopy. The room, however, was merely the setting, for as Myra floated across the floor, Blake was stunned by her beauty as he was each time he saw her. A formfitting, sky-blue dress with tiny pearl buttons accentuated her hourglass shape. Her raven-black hair fell upon her shoulders in large fluffy curls, and her soft blue eyes set off a perfectly chiseled face.

A look passed between Myra and Blake, but it was

only a look and nothing more. There had been times when Blake thought that there could have been something special between them; times when he thought that Myra looked at him in that way, yet she never expressed any interest in him beyond that point. As far as his interest in her was concerned, he had no right to show it. In fact, what would be the point? Such a relationship would be futile, for he was no match in any regard for Max McCargo. Furthermore, ever since Myra had come to town two months ago, McCargo had made it quite clear that he had staked his claim.

"He wants you," Blake stated in a businesslike tone.

Myra's face drained. "When?"

"Tomorrow. I can pick you up and take you to the jail."

"But you said it wouldn't be wise for me to see him."

"It isn't, but he wants you anyway."

Myra lowered her head and wrung her hands. For a moment she did not acknowledge Blake's presence. Finally, she looked up, forced a smile, and said, "All right."

Blake started to say something, thought it best to remain silent, and turned for the door.

Myra took a step forward and placed a trembling hand on Blake's arm. "I–I'm afraid."

Blake eyed her curiously. He felt a sense of sorrow in seeing such a beautiful face marred by sadness and fear. He knew that her emotions were genuine. He wanted to take her into his arms and hold her, to protect her, but he knew that he lacked the courage.

"Are you afraid?" she asked, her eyes looking into his.

"Yes," he said after a long pause.

"When I first came to this town a few months ago, I thought I knew what I wanted. Max McCargo was part of that. Now, I know I was wrong. I made a mistake and I can't walk away from it."

"Max McCargo is a hard man to walk away from. I know a few who tried. They lived to regret it."

"What about you? Did you ever try?"

"What makes you think I ever wanted to?"

"I can tell, somehow I can tell that you're in the same situation that I'm in. You're not the kind of man to do . . . well, what you're doing . . . for Max McCargo or for anyone else."

"I'm afraid, Miss Fontaine, that I'm not much of a man at all."

"How can you talk like that?"

He looked away from her and fingered the brim of his hat. "When you can't look at yourself in the mirror anymore . . . well, you know there's not much left."

"I don't believe that of you. The fact that you're suffering inside tells me otherwise."

"Don't rely too heavily on me, Miss Fontaine. I may prove to be an utter disappointment."

She removed her hand from his arm and exhaled deeply. "If there were any chance, any chance at all, would you take it?" she asked.

He regarded her closely and felt a strange stirring deep within, as though an ember he thought long dead had suddenly sparked again. "If there were any kind of a chance . . . " he said with a frown, "but I don't know that such a possibility even exists."

"What about this man Malverne? Is there anything he can do to stop McCargo?"

"If he were to reach Grand City and testify, his testimony would be unimpeachable."

"Then—"

"But at this moment in time, I doubt that Malverne is still alive. If he is, I can't imagine that there's even one chance in ten—maybe one in twenty—that he can survive the journey."

Chapter Three

It was an hour before dawn when Hawthorne was awakened by a faint scraping sound coming from somewhere behind him. His eyelids quivered, opened slightly, and his eyes located Malverne on the far side of the fire, asleep in his bedroll. One of the horses nickered softly. Without moving a muscle, he listened intently, attempting to gauge distance and exact location. For a full five minutes, he heard nothing. Then, it came again, this time more distinctly. Someone or something was crawling toward him—eight, maybe ten feet away.

He lay on his left side. His gun hand was in front of him, under the blanket, not close enough to his holster to reach his Colt without showing movement. He concluded he had but seconds to assess the situation. It had to be a man. The horses would have reacted more violently to a mountain lion or a bear. He

27

guessed one man—most likely not an Indian. He would not have heard an Indian.

The noise came again. Someone was within a few feet of his back. He had to make his move. Carefully, so as not to tip his hand, he clutched the edge of the blanket with the fingers of his right hand. Taking in a breath to steady himself, he paused for as long as he dared, and then he moved. With his right hand, he flung the blanket into the air. It billowed, like a fisherman's net being cast over water, and fell over a squirming form. Simultaneously, using his left elbow for leverage, he spun around on his hip, pulled in his legs until his knees touched his chin, and shot out his feet with as much force as he could muster. He felt resistance as his boots struck hard at the shapeless form beneath the blanket, and he heard a deep grunt followed by a low moan. In an instant, Hawthorne was on his knees and his gun was in his hand.

A shot erupted from the direction of a deadfall at the edge of the camp. Hawthorne saw the flash and he heard a whine close to his ear. He returned fire, aiming once, then peppering the area around the deadfall by fanning his Colt three times. He heard a noise as though something had fallen in the brush. A groan followed. The gunfire stopped and Hawthorne rose to his feet. Malverne was tucked into a ball near his bedroll, a look of terror on his face made worse by the shadows cast upon him by the flickering campfire. The mule was letting loose with a discordant bray, and the chestnut was snorting wildly, dancing back and forth, arching its head into the air. The bay lay on the ground—dead.

His gun still in his hand, ready, Hawthorne scanned the perimeter of the camp but detected no other sound or movement. He crossed over to the chestnut, patted it down soothingly, and then walked it away from the bay and the smell of blood. He picketed the chestnut and returned to the mule, which continued to bray nervously. Hawthorne stroked its back and walked it around for a few minutes before it finally settled into a more subdued state, although it continued to grunt on and off. Hawthorne secured the mule and then stepped over to the still form under the blanket. He lifted the blanket and tossed it aside, revealing a man who lay on his stomach, his arms outstretched in front of him, a knife inches away from his right hand. Hawthorne picked up the knife and tucked it under his belt. He then patted down the man, turned him over, and peered at his face.

"Silvero," Hawthorne whispered. He pulled a handgun from the man's holster, which he held out to Malverne. "Keep him covered. If he makes a move, drill him."

Malverne, his fear abating, took the gun and nodded. He walked closer to the man and looked down at him. He appeared to be a Mexican. He wore a dirty hat, a serape, and chigaderos. His face was swarthy, he had a thin black mustache, and his lip was bleeding.

Another groaning sound came from the direction of the deadfall. Hawthorne raised his Colt and stated firmly, "Condor! Come out with your hands in the air, or I'll fire again."

After a pause, a voice called out weakly, "Don't shoot, Marshal. You hit me. You killed me for sure."

"Start moving, Condor, or I'll burn powder."

"Cain't, Marshal. I told you I'm wounded."

"Then crawl forward, you yellow-bellied bush-whacker!"

Another groan followed, there was a stirring in the brush, and a big man emerged from the darkness, holding one arm stiffly while he held his other arm in the air. "I'm hurt bad, Marshal. I'll likely bleed to death if I move around any more."

Hawthorne moved toward him cautiously and checked him for weapons. Finding none, he grabbed Condor by the front of his shirt and shoved him toward the fire.

Condor stumbled backward, fell heavily to the ground, and cried out in pain. "You got no call to handle a wounded man like that," he yelped through gritted teeth.

"Keep your mouth shut, you backshooting horse thief," Hawthorne rapped, replacing his Colt in his holster. He disappeared into the brush and emerged carrying a Winchester.

Condor was about fifty, had a scraggly beard and a bull neck. His clothes were worn thin. He had the general look of a hard case. Blood was oozing down his left shirtsleeve. He held his wounded arm with his right hand and considered Hawthorne with a look that blended fear with hatred.

"Who are they? Are they after me?" Malverne asked, his eyes darting back and forth from Condor to Silvero.

"Jud Condor and his partner Silvero. No, it's not likely that they're after you. These boys spend most of their time in the mountains. They don't do much newspaper reading."

"Then what is it that they want?"

"Our horses for one thing. They're horse thieves primarily, but they aren't proud. They're not above rustling a steer or two when the opportunity presents itself. It's more likely they wanted me. I put them away a year ago for trying to steal a horse from a farmer just outside of Spencer. The judge gave the pair of them six months."

"Now, Marshal, me and Silvero didn't know it was you—honest. I admit we had our eyes on your mounts, but we had no plans for hurtin' anybody, and that's gospel."

Hawthorne emptied the spent cartridges from his Colt and inserted new ones. "Is that why Silvero was creeping up on me with his pig-sticker? Just what did he have in mind?"

"I'm sure he just wanted to cut your picket rope."

"Uh huh. And you—firing at me from ambush?"

"Well, Marshal, when you jumped Silvero, well . . . I sorta panicked. I had to protect my partner. You understand?" Condor said, forcing a smile and laughing nervously.

"Sure, I understand," Hawthorne said. He glanced at Silvero, who was out cold. He then knelt down beside Condor and tore the sleeve from his shirt. Condor grimaced in pain. Hawthorne inspected the wound and shook his head. "It's messy but not serious. The slug passed through."

He obtained some bandages from his saddlebags and selected one of the spare canteens from the pack the mule had been toting. As he knelt down beside Condor, the outlaw made a sudden move toward the knife under Hawthorne's belt. Anticipating just such an action, Hawthorne clamped his hand down on Condor's wrist. He held it, squeezing it with a viselike grip until the outlaw shrieked with pain. With his other hand, Hawthorne drew his Colt and swung it down hard on Condor's neck. The outlaw fell over on his back like a sack of grain.

"I'd just as soon have him out when I dress this wound. I couldn't stand his crying. Not only is he a thief, he's a snivelling coward."

Malverne took a deep breath and then let out a sigh of relief as he continued to maintain his watch over Silvero.

It was daybreak by the time Hawthorne finished tending to Condor's wound. The outlaw sat up, groggy and sore. Silvero had also come around. His lip was red and swollen. He glared at Hawthorne with an expression that advertised a deep hatred.

Hawthorne located the outlaws' horses, an apron-faced gray and a coyote dun, a short distance from camp. He led them back and tied them to some brush next to the chestnut. They were hard-wintered mounts, and Hawthorne shook his head as he inspected them.

Turning to Condor and Silvero, he said, "I can see why you boys have to steal horses. What did you do with the ponies?"

Stunned by the question, Condor and Silvero looked at each other in surprise.

"What ponies?" Condor replied.

"I spotted your tracks yesterday. There were two unshod ponies with you."

Silvero smiled. "You are mistaken, senor. We have no ponies," he said in a thick Spanish accent.

Hawthorne pointed to the prints in the dirt at his feet. "That split in the hoof on the right foreleg of that dun is as plain as the welt on your face, Silvero. I saw it yesterday. The two of you were leading a pair of unshod ponies."

Silvero shot a surreptitious glance at Condor.

Condor looked away, stared at the ground at his feet for a long moment, and then slowly nodded his head. "All right. We did have some ponies. They was run off last night by some Shoshones."

"I don't suppose you stole them from the Shoshones to begin with?"

"Well, what if we did? Takin' cayuses from an Indian ain't the same as takin' 'em from a white man. No court would convict us for that, and you know it," Condor said.

"Maybe, but you have to admit that it's kind of funny though."

"Yeah, what's funny about it?"

Hawthorne grinned. "Well, here you sit—the two

biggest horse thieves within a dozen counties—victimized at your own game."

Malverne chuckled.

Silvero muttered something in Spanish, and Condor shot a vicious sneer at Hawthorne.

"But any way that you look at it, you boys can still count this as your lucky day."

"Yeah, and just how do you figure that?" Condor asked.

"Because I'm not placing you under arrest."

The outlaws stared at each other in shocked surprise.

"You mean you ain't takin' us in for what we done?" Condor said.

Hawthorne shook his head. "I don't have the time."

"Then . . . we're free to go?"

"I want the both of you to get out of the state. If I ever see either of you again, I'll drill you without so much as a warning."

"You'll never see us again, Marshal. I can guarantee that."

"Si, senor," Silvero concurred, showing an uneven row of stained teeth as he grinned broadly.

"We'll mount up and be on our way right now. We'll ride and ride far," Condor announced, pushing himself to his feet with his one good arm.

"Not so fast," Hawthorne cautioned.

Condor froze. He stared at Silvero, who stared back, a sudden wave of fear coursing between them.

"I'll be liberating you of that gray," Hawthorne announced. "It isn't much, but I need it."

"But—"

"Your shot took down the bay," Hawthorne said, interrupting Condor, jerking his thumb over his shoulder.

Condor looked at the horse's carcass and ran his hand across his mouth. "We'll never make it out of these mountains on one horse."

"No, but you can make it to Ike Cornstalk's roadhouse. With you riding and Silvero walking, you can get there in seven or eight hours if you push it. From there you can deal. Besides, Ike is a pretty fair hand at doctoring. He can tend that arm better than I did."

"Will you at least give me back my rifle?"

"So you'll have another chance at bushwhacking me?"

"How about a handgun?"

"No gun."

"But there are Indians in these mountains. What chance have we got with no gun, one horse, and me wounded?" Condor pleaded.

"A better one than you gave us when you slithered into our camp," Hawthorne said flatly.

Chapter Four

Mace Gorman leaned against the wall of the telegraph office listening to the rhythmic clicking of the
key. It told a story that he could not read, yet he knew
that the sounds translated into money chinking in his
pocket. Orders from the man. Orders he would exe-
cute—without question, without hesitation, as he always had. Being employed as Max McCargo's top gun
for the last seven years, he knew how to take orders
and how to delegate authority to the other gunmen on
McCargo's payroll. He never asked for reasons or ex-
planations; he merely did as he was told. Furthermore,
he expected others to do the same. Those who knew
him came to realize that it was not a wise policy to
second-guess him. He dealt personally with men of
that leaning, and he meted out his own brand of justice
quickly and harshly.

The clerk passed a telegram to Gorman through the

window, and Gorman began to decipher it. Immediately, he knew it was from Blake. It took but a minute to digest the message, and Gorman stepped into the street and headed for the saloon, where he knew the boys would be waiting over whiskey and cards. At six-feet-four, Gorman carried his two hundred and fifty pounds on a rangy frame. He had a swarthy complexion, vacant eyes, and a large square jaw. He had a preference for dark clothes, and he always wore his shirtsleeves rolled up just below his elbows, thus advertising his massive forearms and giving him total freedom of movement near his handguns. He wore a pair of them, tied down low on his thighs. They were the most salient things about him, promoting his profession, which was, simply put, that of a hired killer. There was nothing subtle about Mace Gorman. He was blunt, callous, and plain spoken. One might liken him to a locomotive that ran on only one track. Since no man had ever been able to derail him, he had no reason to be anything but blunt, callous, and plainspoken.

He crossed the street, stepped onto the boardwalk, and passed through the swinging doors of the saloon, where he stood for a moment as he took in the scene. His size alone was reason for everyone to give pause and look up from whatever it was he was doing. He nodded to his men, and they immediately rose from their seats, followed him to an isolated table, and clustered around him.

A few others who were standing at the bar got a sense of what was happening. They knocked down their drinks and drifted out the door.

Gorman seemed to tower over the other men by a head. As he leaned forward to rest his hands on the back of a chair, the muscles of his huge forearms flexed beneath his weight.

"New orders, Gorman?" one of the men asked.

Gorman nodded. "Mr. McCargo wants every town between the capital and Grand City covered. He wants this territory bottled up tighter than a jug of corn liquor."

"Any news as to Malverne's location?"

"Nope. Malverne could be almost anywhere. He could be approaching Grand City from any direction. It doesn't matter. He won't get through."

"How do you want the men divided?" Avery Truman asked.

Gorman removed a map from his shirt pocket. He unfolded it and placed it on the table in front of him. As the others moved in for a closer look, he divided the men into pairs and assigned them specific locations. Avery Truman, Gorman's second in command, would relay additional directions to others along the route. Using the telegraph as well as riders, a coordinated effort would be put into place to draw a tight circle around Grand City itself. In addition to the towns along the route—as well as those even remotely in the vicinity of the route—every road and stage line would be covered. Given the manpower at his disposal, it would be virtually impossible for Malverne to slip through Gorman's circle undetected.

Following the briefing, Gorman looked at the faces of the men encircling him. "One more thing, boys. Mr.

McCargo has just upped the bounty on Malverne. The man who puts a slug in him will earn himself twenty-thousand dollars."

One of the men gasped; another let out a low whistle. Most of them were speechless.

"That's more money than most men earn in a lifetime," Truman said.

Gorman picked up a bottle and poured a round of drinks. "Yeah, that's a handful of money all right, but just remember this. Mr. McCargo wants that squealin' weasel stomped on, and so do I . . . and any of you jackals that lets Malverne slip through his fingers will answer to me . . . and when I get done with him, there won't be enough for Mr. McCargo to spit on."

Gorman emptied his shot glass, turned away without another word, and walked out of the saloon. The others broke up in silence.

An hour later Gorman was sitting alone at a table in the only restaurant in town. He had just finished a beefsteak, a plate of beans, and a pot of coffee. As he stared out the grimy window overlooking the main street, he thought about the twenty-thousand-dollar bounty McCargo was offering. Truman was right. It was more wages than a man was likely to earn in a lifetime. Gorman speculated on what he would do with such an enormous sum should he get his hands on it. He had no interest in land. Although he was raised on a ranch in Texas, he never enjoyed doing ranch chores much less being around cattle. He was no farmer and possessed no business skills. The only things he had ever been good with were his fists and his guns, and working for such a powerful man as McCargo had given him a license to use both and get away with it.

He had fallen into the ideal situation as top gun for Maximilian McCargo. In fact, he owed everything he had to the man. In his younger days, he had gotten into one scrape after another with the law. Saloon brawls, drunkenness, and gunfights had scarred his past. He had left a trail of destruction from one state to another as he drifted further and further west, often one step ahead of the law. It was in Colorado where he had first met McCargo. McCargo was just getting started then—in cattle. He was land-hungry; he had an unquenchable thirst for money and power, which Gorman recognized at once, for he had seen such a fever before, burning in many men he had encountered in his travels across the country. Gorman had had a dispute with a pair of ranch hands over a saloon girl in a town whose name he could not even remember. He shot it out with them, wounding one badly and killing the other. Although most of the onlookers claimed that Gorman had provoked the fight, McCargo intervened on his behalf, saving him from a rope.

McCargo's money and influence were more than enough to sway public empathy in a small cow town to get Gorman off with a fine and a promise to leave the county. From that day on, Gorman was on McCargo's payroll, and from that day on, he had been loyal to a fault. Gorman decided long ago that he would remain loyal—regardless of where it would take him.

He was not above doing dirty work, for he was paid

well for his services. He had saved nearly $5,000, most of which was deposited in the Grand City Bank. With an additional $20,000, he would have the opportunity to retire and live in comfort for the rest of his life. Mexico was a possibility. He could live the life of an aristocrat south of the border with that kind of a bankroll. He had even heard stories about South America, where a man could disappear and live down his past. Gorman drained his cup and pushed himself away from the table, his thoughts consumed with exciting possibilities of wealth and comfort.

Twenty minutes later Gorman was in his hotel room packing his saddlebags when he heard a knock at the door. Checking his guns, he strolled across the room and turned the knob.

"I understand you're looking for a man."

Gorman stared at a solitary figure in the hallway. After a long moment, he nodded and stepped aside. The figure entered the room, and Gorman closed the door.

By mid-morning Hawthorne and Malverne had pushed past the tree line, abandoning the pines and firs for more open spaces. Now, the land was stark and barren, characterized by sharp, jagged rocks and little vegetation. The sun was hot, and they paused frequently to water the animals wherever streams presented themselves and to assess the land around them. Hawthorne was more vigilant now, for cover and concealment were no longer in their favor should they come under attack. He fished his spyglass from his saddlebags often, checking the terrain before them as well as their back trail. Since their encounter with the horse thieves, Condor and Silvero, they had seen no sign of anyone—white man or Indian. Such a situation was exactly to Hawthorne's liking, for that was his reason for selecting this particular route. The longer he could isolate Malverne the better his chances of keeping him alive. Loose lips could prove fatal, and Hawthorne had no intention of taking any unnecessary risks.

It was late afternoon when they came upon a small stream that flowed from a deep crevice in a crag of rock. It gathered into a large pool, where they filled their canteens, washed, and watered the horses and the mule.

Malverne soaked his bandanna in the cool water and placed it over his face as he sat with his back against the rock. Hawthorne scanned the area again before selecting a shady spot and stretching out his legs. As he checked his Colt, he spotted something shiny in the sand beside him. He picked it up and brushed it clean. It was a small gold locket with a thin chain that had broken through. It opened with a click, revealing a pair of pictures. One was unmistakably Malverne. His hair was neatly plastered, and he wore a suit and tie. The other was a lady. She had dark brown hair, rather a plain face, and a pleasant smile. Hawthorne studied the pictures for a while and then shut the locket.

"Malverne."

Malverne pulled the bandanna from his face and looked up.

Hawthorne tossed the locket to him, which Malverne caught in midair.

"The chain broke. I found it here in the sand."

Malverne nodded. He opened the locket, stared at it for a long moment, and then shut it securely. He held it tightly in his hand for some time and then carefully tucked it inside his pants pocket. As he looked up, he noticed that Hawthorne's eyes were fixed on him.

After a long pause, Malverne said, "Her name was Sara Bleeker, and she's the reason why I'm here now, baking in the sun, probably on my way to my own execution."

Hawthorne did not respond. He remained silent, giving more rope to Malverne in the hope that he would speak out. He had never made any inquiries of Malverne during their journey, and Malverne had been taciturn about his testimony, to say nothing of his background. The discovery of the locket, however, had piqued Hawthorne's curiosity, and he was, admittedly, somewhat anxious to hear about this woman whose picture Malverne carried about with him.

"Your woman?"

"She might have been."

Hawthorne digested Malverne's reply but remained silent, waiting to hear more.

"She came to Grand City for the first time last year—from back East. She was an only child. When her father died, she had no one close, only a cousin who worked as a dressmaker in Grand City. The cousin wrote to her, inviting Sara to stay with her. Sara had never been west before. She wasn't familiar with the ways of the frontier." He smiled. "I remember she had never seen a saloon before or a roundup or a cattle drive. She didn't know much.

"I met her for the first time when I ran into her—literally—outside the Wells Fargo office. She had just gotten off the stage. She looked so scared, so innocent—like a fawn that had gotten separated from its mother for the first time." Malverne chuckled. "Well, I introduced myself and escorted her to the dress shop. As it turned out, her cousin was out of town until the next day. I carried her bags to the hotel and saw that she got a room. It was a nice, simple meeting between two people.

"I called on her the next day, at the dress shop, and asked her to lunch. She accepted and we had a pleasant meal at the hotel. You know, to this day, I can't remember what I ordered. I was just so taken with Sara."

He picked up a pebble and tossed it into the pool. As he watched the ripples disappear, he added, "I'm not a man who's attractive to women. Most of them don't even give me the time of day. Sara was . . . well, by most standards I suppose, plain in appearance. Yet I found something in her that was wonderful. I could tell at once that she was special, and to me she was beautiful. Maybe it was the way she looked at me, the way she paid attention to me as if I were someone important. No one ever treated me like that before. She was kind, generous, and gentle. I had never met anyone like her before, and she seemed to be genuinely interested in me—a little man, an insignificant little man who spent his time writing numbers in ledgers."

"There are worse ways for a man to earn a living," Hawthorne put in.

Malverne nodded. "True, but by most standards, it's been a dull life—certainly not the kind of life that would attract a woman."

"But Sara was attracted to you?"

"She was, and I can't say I know the reason why. We would meet, and talk, and have dinner. We went on picnics; sometimes we just took walks. It was a wonderful time of my life—the most wonderful, I imagine." Malverne stared at a trail of amber ants crawling around a rock at his feet. "I got to know her well . . . I thought I knew her as well as anyone I had ever met. For the first time in my life, I was confident about myself and in what I was doing. I knew I wanted to marry her. I picked the perfect evening to propose to her. We had dinner, champagne. Everything was right. I walked her home, and I told her that I loved her. I asked her to be my wife. She looked at me with those gentle eyes of hers. It was those eyes. They seemed to be able to read my innermost thoughts. She smiled and she squeezed my hand. She kissed me and she said she would be mine. I was never so happy in my life as I was at that minute." Malverne paused, hesitant about continuing.

"Go on," Hawthorne urged.

Malverne's brow furrowed. "By some chance, by some out-of-the-way chance, Sara met Mr. McCargo.

He didn't seem to be at all interested in her. In fact, he didn't even seem to take notice of her, but somehow, in some unexplainable way, he turned her away from me. It wasn't as though he loved her. That would've been different, but Mr. McCargo is incapable of loving anyone but himself. Besides, he has all the women he wants—showgirls, saloon girls. The most attractive women line up to meet him. What would he have wanted with Sara? A man of wealth, power, and influence attracted to a common girl who worked in a dress shop? The whole idea was insane. Sara wasn't for him. It wasn't that at all. It's just that Mr. McCargo enjoys taking things away from other people. Land, cattle, women—whatever he wants, he takes. That's the way it is with him. That's the way it's always been. It isn't as though he needs what he takes. He doesn't. He just wants what belongs to other people. When I first started working for him, I was too blind to realize it. Then, after a while, I guess I didn't want to believe it, maybe because the money was too good, or I was too deeply involved. I don't know. After a time, I guess it was just too late, but I never figured that Sara could ever be one of his . . . acquisitions."

"Sara ran off with him?"

Malverne laughed. "I only wish that she had. I'd have an easier time living with myself if she had." He wiped his face with his bandanna, rolled it, and placed it around his neck again. "One night I called on Sara. We had agreed to have dinner, and I was anxious to see her. Her cousin answered the door. She told me that Sara wasn't feeling well and had retired. Her cousin was a poor actress. She couldn't even look me in the face. I could tell at a glance that she was lying. I went home upset. I barely slept that night. Early the next morning I went directly to the dress shop. Sara wasn't there, and her cousin told me that she was still sick. I went to the house, knocked on the door, but there was no answer. I knocked louder and called out Sara's name. Again, there was no response. I became concerned. I shouted at the top of my voice, threatening to kick in the door. Finally, Sara appeared. It was obvious that she had been crying. I took her in my arms and asked her what was wrong. She refused to discuss the matter with me and asked me to leave. I asked her what I had done to offend her, knowing full well that I hadn't done anything. She wouldn't talk to me. She wouldn't even look at me. When I pressed her further for an explanation, she pushed away from me, buried her face in her hands and began to cry.

"I pleaded for several minutes and finally got her to face me. She began asking me over and over to forgive her. I didn't know what she was talking about. I encouraged her as gently as I could to explain what she meant." Malverne bit his lip. "I should never have found out. Her eyes betrayed her. Somehow I knew before the words even came from her lips. She had been with Mr. McCargo.

"She said that she didn't know why she had done such a thing. She had no explanation for it. She had never done anything like it before. When she was through confessing everything to me, she begged me to forgive her. I couldn't believe what she was telling me. I couldn't even utter a word. Just as her eyes betrayed her to me, the expression on my face must have betrayed me to her. She got a look of fear on her face. She clutched at me with a strength I didn't know she had, but I managed to tear myself from her and walk away.

"It was then that I knew what I had to do. I returned to my room and dug out an old derringer that I bought when I first came west. I had never used it before, wasn't even certain how to load it, but then I wasn't exactly thinking clearly. I made my way to Mr. McCargo's office, walked in, and pulled out the gun. He stood there, puffing at his cigar, an amused look on his face.

"To this day, I don't know whether or not I could've pulled the trigger. It didn't matter. Mace Gorman was there. I didn't even notice him when I entered. Before I even had my say, Gorman grabbed my wrist, and took the gun from my hand as easily as if he had picked an apple off a tree. He tweaked my nose so hard that my eyes watered; I lost my balance and fell to the floor. Both men stood there and laughed at me as if I were a badly behaved child who'd been punished. Mr. McCargo told Gorman to return my derringer. He knew I wouldn't be able to use it. He told me to go back to my office and work on my ledgers. Gorman picked me up, crammed the derringer into my vest pocket, and shoved me out of the room.

"I went back to my books as I was told, and I stayed there. For the next two days, I buried myself in my work, avoiding Sara. I went nowhere near her cousin's house or the dress shop. I didn't know what to do. I didn't know what to say to her if I saw her. I couldn't eat. I slept only a few hours. My nerves were shot. It took me until the third day before I knew what I had to do. I loved Sara. No matter what might have happened, I knew I still loved her with all my heart. I still wanted to marry her. I was determined to see her and tell her that, and I believed with all my heart that we could make it work. She had asked for my forgiveness. I could forgive her. It didn't matter to me. I had to tell her that. I had to tell her again that I loved her.

"I went immediately to the dress shop, but I was surprised to find it closed. I hurried to her cousin's house. When I got there, I found her cousin in tears. I knew right away that something was very wrong. Sara was dead. She had taken poison during the night. Next to her was a note which she had left for me. In it she wrote that she loved me, but she believed that I could never forgive her."

Hawthorne had listened intently to Malverne's story, but for the first time he could not look at him. His eyes trailed away to the pool where he watched the water trickle from the rock, gently disrupting the surface.

Chapter Five

Hawthorne was not surprised when Malverne'e
gray came up lame. He had been favoring his right
foreleg for several miles. Hawthorne cursed Condor
and Silvero under his breath as he dismounted to
check on the beleaguered animal. He was amazed that
it had gotten this far, scrawny as it was.

"Is it bad?" Malverne asked.

"I'm afraid it is. We've already pushed him too far
for the condition he's in. He won't be able to hold
your weight any longer."

"What now? Do we walk?"

"We have no choice."

"I was being sarcastic. You can't be serious," Malverne added, a stunned expression on his face.

"It's only a few more miles to the Buttermilk place.
That's our destination anyway. Both horses can use a
breather, and we can get fresh mounts there."

"All right," Malverne said reluctantly as he eased himself out of the saddle.

Hawthorne gently patted the gray on the flank as he removed the saddle and secured it atop his own. The gray limped painfully as Hawthorne walked slowly in front of him, leading him by the reins, pausing occasionally to add words of encouragement and to pat the struggling animal.

For more than an hour, the gray managed with a courage that belied his sorry appearance. Hawthorne halted the mounts a quarter of a mile from the Buttermilk ranch house and assessed the terrain with a cautious eye. The lay of the land was exactly the way he had remembered it when he was last here, some four weeks ago. The ranch house was constructed of stone. It had been built by Cal Buttermilk with meticulous concern—three walls abutting the side of a mountain of rock. A thin wisp of smoke curled up from the fireplace and disappeared among the steep ledges above. A hundred feet away were a barn, a tack room, and a lean-to. Several corrals of various sizes were positioned nearby, most of which were home to some half a dozen horses. Cal Buttermilk had lived here for nearly forty years. He had made his livelihood capturing wild horses, breaking them, and selling them. He also did a fair share of trading and some horse doctoring. Hawthorne had known him for a major portion of his life. He worked for Buttermilk the summer of his seventeenth year. In place of wages, he received room and board and his pick from the herd of wild horses which Buttermilk brought in. More important, however, than the horse, was the know-how he had gained from his association with the man who knew more about horseflesh than anyone he had ever met.

Buttermilk was coming out of the barn as Hawthorne and Malverne approached the outer corral. He stopped in his tracks and stared for a long moment; then, upon recognizing Hawthorne, he waved and ambled toward them.

Buttermilk looked to be about sixty-five. He was short, not more than five-six or five-seven, but his ten-gallon hat magnified his stature. He was bowlegged, and he limped badly on his left leg. His face and arms were bronzed from the sun. He seemed to be bone and sinew, with little flesh to spare. It was obvious that the horse trade had kept him fit and hardy even at his age.

"Why, Trace, I didn't expect to see you until tomorrow or thereabouts," he said, removing his sweat-stained hat and using it to fan some of the dust from his clothes.

"We made better time than I thought until this old beggar pulled up lame."

Shooting a glance at the gray, Buttermilk shook his head. "Since when have you been ridin' disreputable-lookin' sways like that? And why did you bring him here? Do you want to give this place a bad name?"

"It's a long story. I'll tell you all about it later. This is Mr. Malverne—the guest I told you about."

Malverne and Buttermilk shook hands. Malverne felt a firm grip that left his hand stinging.

"Pleased to meet up with you, sir. My home is your home."

"Thanks," Malverne replied, smiling slightly as he eyed the ranch house.

"Oh, it ain't much to look at, but it's sturdy enough, and it's been home to me since I was twenty-five. Got a treat for you boys, too. My niece Lane is livin' here now. She moved in with me since her pa died. So you boys don't have to tolerate my cookin'."

"Thank the Lord for that," Hawthorne said, grinning.

Buttermilk burst out laughing.

"It's good to see you again, Cal," Hawthorne added, extending his hand.

Buttermilk took it and pumped it vigorously. "It's good to see you again, boy, real good! You don't get by as often as I'd like. I know that you're here now on business, but we can still try to have us some social time."

"Sure we can."

"Oh, 'afore I forget, this telegram came yesterday." Buttermilk patted down his shirt pockets before he finally fished a piece of paper from one of his rear pants pockets. "I picked it up when I was in town buyin' supplies. It was sent to me, but I reckon it was meant for you, seein' as how you told me you might be gettin' messages through me."

"Why don't you read it, seeing as how you probably already have."

Buttermilk grinned. "All right. You know, this message could've been meant for me the way it was written."

"That's because it's in a special code so that anyone who happened to read it wouldn't think twice if it was sent to you."

"I see. I see. Well, let me read it then. It says: Lead stallion and one mare lost during raid by bandits. You must deliver replacement by specified time. G."

Hawthorne's face suddenly turned sullen.

When Buttermilk looked at him, his grin dissolved. "Just what does it all mean, boy?"

Hawthorne wrapped his hand around one of the corral posts and dropped his head.

Buttermilk and Malverne stared at him, startled by the sudden change in him.

Hawthorne tugged at his Stetson and breathed deeply. "The morning after Malverne and I began our journey, another man set out for Grand City. He was similar to Malverne in stature and appearance. He had six armed guards with him."

"A decoy?" Buttermilk asked.

"Yes. Everything was done openly, including a show of force. We knew that another attempt would be made on your life, Malverne, but we were on the alert this time, with a number of capable gunhands. Our men succeeded in drawing attention away from us. Thanks to them no one knows where we are, but the price was higher than I hoped it would be."

"You mean the stallion and the mare . . . mean two men?" Malverne asked.

"Yes. The stallion—the man posing as you—was a

lawman named Jim Wells. He was my deputy for the last two years and my friend for the last six. He was twenty-eight years old. He had a wife and two small sons."

Malverne tried hard to swallow but could not. "What a waste. What a waste of life."

Hawthorne's eyes fixed on him coldly. "Don't ever say that. Jim Wells wore a badge, and he believed in what it stood for. He died for what he believed in, and there's no waste in that."

"I just hope I'm worth it," Malverne said dejectedly.

"I don't know whether you are or not, Malverne, but there are plenty of good men, including the governor of this state, who are willing to lay their lives on the line because of you. I've got the feeling that there will be others—some good, some bad—who will end up in the dust before this is over, but no matter what it takes, I'm going to get you to that courtroom, and you're going to give testimony against McCargo."

"Did you say the governor? You mean the 'G' on this telegram stands for the governor?" Buttermilk asked.

"That's right. He's the only one who knows where we are right now. I'm afraid that there are men around him, men close to him that he can't trust."

Buttermilk ran his hand across his mouth.

"But what's the difference if they don't know where we are?" Malverne put in. "We still have to go to Grand City, and they know that. We have to go to Mr. McCargo, and all they have to do is wait."

A slight smile formed on Hawthorne's face. "Maybe

... maybe not. Maybe we can work it so McCargo comes to us."

Malverne stared at him quizzically.

"Supper's ready, Uncle Cal."

The men turned to see a young woman of about twenty-one. She wore a plaid shirt, denims, and boots. Her shoulder-length hair was the color of wheat, her eyes were large and brown, and her cheekbones were high. The only thing which flawed her otherwise perfectly formed face was a slight bump on the bridge of her nose, suggesting that her nose had been broken some time long ago.

"Oh, Lane, our guests arrived earlier then expected."

"That's all right, Uncle Cal. There's plenty of food," she announced, her eyes flitting back and forth between Hawthorne and Malverne.

"Good. This is Marshal Trace Hawthorne."

Hawthorne touched the brim of his Stetson.

"Welcome, Marshal," she said with a slight blush.

"And Mr. Malverne."

"Miss," Malverne said, nodding.

"Mr. Malverne."

"Gents, this is my niece, Lane Carter," Buttermilk stated proudly.

Hawthorne thought that she was the prettiest girl he had ever seen. In fact, there was only one other who could have rivaled her, a stage singer he had seen in Denver when he was nineteen, and she was fancy dressed in a gown that sparkled, and she wore many jewels.

"Why don't you boys wash up while I tend to your stock," Buttermilk suggested.

Hawthorne nodded, and he and Malverne followed Lane to the house. There was a bench on a stone porch with a basin of water, soap, and towels. The men brushed some of the trail dust from their clothes and cleaned up while Lane made her way inside. Ten minutes later Hawthorne and Malverne entered the house. It had changed little since Hawthorne had first seen it when he was seventeen—except that now it was swept and tidy, and there were some pretty curtains hanging over the windows, no doubt some of Lane's recent touches. They were greeted by a large room filled with chairs that were worn but comfortable-looking, some small side tables, a few throw rugs, and some framed paintings of mountains and horses. A cabinet filled with plates and cups covered a large section of one wall. Off to the left was a dinner table prepared for four. Just beyond was a massive stone fireplace in which a cheery fire was burning. An adjacent room served as the kitchen, from which Lane emerged, carrying plates of steaming stew which she placed on the table.

"Please sit down, gentlemen," she said as she disappeared again, only to reappear a moment later with a gigantic coffeepot and a heaping plate of cornbread.

As Hawthorne and Malverne sat down, Lane filled their cups and hovered over them solicitously, asking if they required anything and seeing to their every need. Hawthorne noticed that not only had she changed her shirt to a blue blouse, but she had also run a brush through her hair. He wondered when she had had the opportunity to make such improvements and finish readying the supper in so short a time.

The men ate heartily for several minutes without talking, for they were hungry and it was the finest food they had eaten since they had begun their journey. In a while Buttermilk entered, placed his hat on a wall peg, and sat down beside the others. He helped himself to a healthy piece of cornbread, dipped it into his stew, and swallowed it in three bites.

"I swear, I believe I've put on seven pounds since Lane's been here," Buttermilk proclaimed.

"It's the best cooking I've had in a month, Lane," Hawthorne announced, and Malverne nodded in agreement.

Lane beamed proudly. "You boys are just hungry."

"Hunger's got nothin' to do with fine vittles, niece," Buttermilk added, reaching for another piece of cornbread.

The four of them exchanged pleasantries about the food before Hawthorne changed the subject.

"I'm sorry to hear about your pa, Lane. I believe I met him once some years ago. Railroad man, wasn't he?"

"Yes, he was, Marshal. He was sick for quite a spell before he passed on," she said, a little moisture forming in her eyes.

"Lane took care of him 'til the end, Trace. She's a fine girl. She may be headin' back East soon to live with kin in Iowa."

"Oh?"

Lane shrugged her shoulders. "I haven't decided yet. I've spent my whole life in this part of the country. I don't really want to leave it."

"Keepin' house for a run-down uncle on an old horse ranch ain't a satisfactory life for a pretty young gal," Buttermilk managed to say between huge bites of meat and potatoes.

"Oh, it isn't that bad. Uncle Cal is sweet enough."

"Your uncle's right, Lane. It isn't good to be alone, isolated," Malverne said.

"We get into town twice a week, and I have a few friends there that I get to see. If I went back to Iowa, I wouldn't know anyone at all. The thought of that is a little scary to me," she returned, sipping at her coffee.

"Makin' new friends is the easiest thing in the world, especially for a good person like you," Buttermilk said.

Lane blushed.

"He's right," Malverne added. "You're young and you've got your whole life before you. Don't be afraid to take some chances. You have to when you're young. When you get older, you start to run scared. You're afraid to make changes. Don't wait so long that life passes you by."

The three of them looked at Malverne, who stared sadly at the cup in front of him.

The conversation meandered through several topics as the men enjoyed a second helping of everything. Finally, Lane stood up and started to clear the table.

"I hope you've all saved room for dessert. I made a fresh apple pie this morning."

The men looked at each other and nodded. Lane finished tidying up the table before bringing in more plates and the pie, which she divided into three pieces. As the men dug into the flaky crust, she refilled their cups. She chose just to sip at her coffee and watch the men enjoy the pastry.

Twenty minutes later, Lane was busy in the kitchen. Malverne sank into one of the big chairs and started to doze off. Buttermilk nudged Hawthorne and said, "I always like to get some fresh air after supper. Wanna stroll out to the corral?"

Hawthorne nodded and the pair picked up their Stetsons and made their way past the barn to the corral with the largest number of horses. They leaned over the top rail and eyed the animals.

"Fine bunch you've got, Cal. That bay looks pretty solid."

Buttermilk nodded.

Hawthorne tried to make additional conversation, but Buttermilk's monosyllabic replies alerted him that something was bothering the old-timer.

Finally, Buttermilk said, "That bad wing o' Malverne's—how did he come by it?"

Hawthorne briefly related the circumstances.

Buttermilk bit his lip. "Son, I don't read the newspapers regular. I don't know much about what's goin' on. I just know that this Malverne is supposed to speak up in court so that this McCargo gets what he's got comin'."

"That's about it in a nutshell."

"This McCargo business—it's pretty bad, isn't it?"

"It's bad."

Buttermilk shook his head. "Yeah, that's what I was afraid of. Just when was it you were plannin' on leavin'?"

"Tomorrow at sunup."

"I think you'd better leave tonight."

Hawthorne considered him closely. "Why?"

"Because they'll be here tomorrow—early most likely."

"Who?"

"A man named Gorman and his pack o' coyotes."

Hawthorne pushed himself away from the corral and squared himself against Buttermilk. "Just what is it you know about Gorman?"

"I know he works for McCargo, and I know he's tryin' to stop Malverne from reachin' Grand City. That, just about everybody in the state knows."

"What makes you think Gorman's headed here?"

"Because I told him you'd be here."

Not easily stunned, Hawthorne's jaw dropped.

"That's right, boy, I'm the one who told him. I sold you out . . . for money."

"I don't believe it. You're the one man I thought I could trust," Hawthorne stated, his eyes searching Buttermilk's face for answers.

"I'm sorry, Trace. I know what I did was wrong."

"But you'd never—"

"It's because o' this," Buttermilk announced, tapping his chest with his thumb. "I've got a bum ticker.

The doc gives me a month or two longer before it starts to play out. Then, it could be a matter of a few days or a few hours."

Hawthorne stared at him in sadness and disbelief.

"I wanted to leave something to Lane. Believe it or not, all these years o' breakin' cayuses left me with a bad leg, a bum ticker, and only a few hundred dollars in my bank account. Lane nursed her pa for nearly a year before he died. It was hard on her. I don't want her hangin' about doin' the same for me. And who knows? I might linger longer than the doc says before they bury me under."

"Lane doesn't know?"

"No. That's why I've been proddin' her to go East. If she found out, she'd never leave whilst I was still breathin'. They promised me five-thousand dollars if I told them where you were. I figured that would give Lane a good start in Iowa. They said there'd be no trouble, that they'd just keep you pinned down for a few days so that you couldn't keep that court meetin'. I made 'em promise that no one would get hurt."

"And you believed that?"

Buttermilk frowned. "No, not anymore, not after I saw Malverne's arm in a sling; not after you told me what that telegram really meant. But it doesn't really matter. Gettin' here early the way you did, you can clear out before they arrive. You see, I told 'em you weren't expected until tomorrow."

"Well, that's something anyway." Hawthorne struck the corral rail with his fist.

"I know I let you down, son, but you gotta believe

I never meant for anyone to get hurt. If you don't believe that, then I won't be able to go on livin' with myself."

Slowly, Hawthorne nodded. "I believe you, Cal."

Buttermilk's lips quivered as he brushed a shaky hand across his mouth. "The Lord bless you, son."

"We'd better get moving. You get Lane ready. It will be better coming from you than from me."

"What . . . what do you mean? We're not goin' anywhere."

"Mace Gorman's a killer. What do you think is going to happen when he finds out you've double-crossed him?"

"Well, I reckon—"

"I'll tell you. He'll kill you. And there's no telling what he may do to Lane."

"I could tell him that you didn't show up. He'd never know the difference."

"Do you think he'd believe that?" Hawthorne asked.

"He might."

"Are you willing to gamble Lane's life on it?"

A sick expression formed on Buttermilk's face as he pushed his hands into his pockets and stared at the ground at his feet in stark realization. "No," he said.

"It's best that we're all long gone before Gorman and his men arrive."

"I guess I really did it this time."

"Yeah, you did."

Buttermilk kicked the dirt with his boot. "I'll throw some belongings together, and I'll have Lane rustle up some grub." As he turned and started to walk back toward the house, he felt Hawthorne's hand close firmly around his arm. "What—"

"Don't bother."

He regarded Hawthorne with surprise. "What do you mean? Why not?"

"Because they're already here."

Chapter Six

Buttermilk's face turned ashen.

"Don't look around, just act natural," Hawthorne said in a calm voice. "Pick up that hackamore off the corral post and drift toward the barn. I'll follow a few paces behind."

Buttermilk nodded and did as he was told, although he fumbled a bit when he reached for the hackamore.

Hawthorne removed his Stetson, wiped his brow with his shirtsleeve, and fell into a casual stroll behind Buttermilk.

When Buttermilk reached the front of the barn, Hawthorne spoke to him from behind. "Don't enter the barn. Keep walking in a direct line toward the house. From where they are now, the barn will block their view of us until we're nearly on the front porch."

Buttermilk did not acknowledge Hawthorne's directions, but he obeyed them to the letter as he sauntered past the barn door without turning around.

Hawthorne's right hand moved naturally toward his holster, and he loosened the thong on the hammer of his Colt. He knew it would be futile to stand and fight in the open. Furthermore, if he and Buttermilk took refuge in the barn, they would be separated from Malverne and Lane, who would be virtually defenseless. Their best chance—and the best chance for Malverne and Lane—lay in their reaching the ranch house.

Hawthorne knew that the attack would come as soon as Gorman and his men established their positions. He hoped that he and Buttermilk could reach the house before then, but it was not meant to be. Buttermilk had just stepped onto the porch when the first slug struck the stone facing of the house. A second slug tore away a splinter the size of a man's fist from one of the posts that supported the overhang. It was either the third or the fourth that struck Buttermilk in the back, knocking him off his feet. In an instant, Hawthorne leaped onto the porch, flung open the door, and dragged Buttermilk's limp body into the ranch house. A hail of bullets followed, striking the door frame and penetrating the interior of the house, shattering dishes on the cabinet and splintering the rocky side of the mountain that formed the fourth wall of the house.

Hawthorne saw men near the corral, moving on foot past the barn. They were crouched low to the ground, firing rifles and handguns as they approached. Three of them were bunched together. Hawthorne drew his

Colt and fired three times in rapid succession before he slammed the door shut. Quickly, he moved to one of the windows, opened it, and stood off to the side. There was a lull in the firing, and Hawthorne saw two men on the ground and another being helped to cover by two more. They'll think twice before they rush the house now, he thought.

Hawthorne heard Lane scream, and he turned to see her rushing to Buttermilk's side. She was in a panic at the sight of her uncle lying on the floor, blood pouring out of his back. Malverne rushed to her, put his arm around her, and tried to settle her.

"Get some bandages. Try to stop the bleeding," Hawthorne instructed.

Lane looked up at him, his words failing to register for a moment, and then she nodded her understanding and ran toward a cabinet. She pulled out some cloth, shredded it, and rushed back to Buttermilk. Malverne helped her the best he could.

Hawthorne surveyed the area in front of the ranch house. The men had suddenly taken cover, disappearing from his view. He could not estimate how many there were, but he had seen at least half a dozen riders before he and Buttermilk made for the ranch house. He figured there must be more, many more. Keeping his eyes on the ground around the barn and corrals, he cleared the spent cartridges from his Colt and reloaded. Without turning away, he asked, "How's Cal doing?"

"Not good. I don't think he's breathing," Lane said, choking on her words.

"He's breathing," Malverne said, "but just barely."

"Just try to stop the bleeding. That's all we can do for him for now."

"Who's out there? Why would anyone want to hurt Uncle Cal?" Lane asked in a pleading voice.

"I'm afraid they're after me. I'm the one they want dead," Malverne said, a guilty look on his face as he watched the tears trickling down Lane's cheeks.

"It's about that big trial, isn't it?" she asked.

Malverne nodded.

"Those men out there are going to kill us all, aren't they?"

"Maybe not, Lane. What they want most is to prevent Malverne from testifying. They might settle for keeping us pinned down for a few days."

"If that's true, why did they shoot Uncle Cal?"

Hawthorne and Malverne exchanged glances.

"You're not a very good liar, Marshal," she said.

Hawthorne smiled. "No, I guess I'm not."

Lane ran her hand through her hair. She breathed deeply as she held the cloth in place over Buttermilk's wound. "Oh, if we could only get him to a doctor."

"Lane."

Lane did not look up until Hawthorne repeated her name.

"Lane, are there any other doors or windows besides the ones in this room?"

"No."

"Malverne, secure the shutters on the other window and drop the bar on the door."

Malverne nodded and did as he was told. He then

moved to Hawthorne's side and peeked out the window. "What do you think they'll do now?" he asked.

"I don't know. Probably scatter the horses. Without mounts, we've failed for certain."

"Looks like you got a couple of them."

Hawthorne nodded. "Unfortunately, there are plenty more."

"Yeah. Guns come cheap."

"This Mace Gorman. A big man who rides a big paint?"

"That's him."

"I think I caught a glimpse of him just before the shooting started."

Malverne shuddered. "If he's out there, we're just as good as dead."

"Well, we're not dead yet. See if there are any more guns around here."

After a quick search, Malverne located a Winchester, a Colt .45, and a box of shells near the fireplace.

"I'm not going to be much help with my arm in this sling. Even with two good arms, I might not be able to hit that barn."

"Your job is to testify. Mine is to get you to court. Leave the gunplay to me."

"Right about now that job looks like a tall order."

"It's what I'm paid for." He glanced at Lane. "Do what you can to help her with the old man."

"Right."

Suddenly, a shot rang out, shattering the window, showering glass over the floor. A barrage of shots followed, peppering the house, riddling it like metal hornets attacking in anger. Because the house was constructed of stone, the bullets could not penetrate except at the window, where lead flowed freely.

Hawthorne could only stand by helplessly, for it would be suicidal even to approach the open window.

For a full minute the onslaught continued. Although the stone walls provided adequate protection, there was the fear of bullets fragmenting off the rock wall formed by the mountain. All they could do was stay low to the floor and pray that they would not be victimized by ricocheting slugs. The din was deafening, and when it ceased, the ranch house floor was littered with rock chips, shattered glass from the window and a lamp, and a splintered chair.

Lane and Malverne had done their best to shield Buttermilk from the flying debris.

Cautiously, Hawthorne rose to his feet. The sounds of whinnying and the thumping of horses' hooves alerted him to activity outside. He chanced a look through the window and saw the last of the horses being driven out of the corrals. He had known Gorman's intent, but he had been helpless to do anything to stop him. Hawthorne suspected what Gorman's next move would be, and he feared the worst, for he knew he was so heavily outmanned and outgunned that he would have little chance of instituting any kind of defense against such odds. Gorman's next move would be preceded by another barrage of firepower. Hawthorne figured that his best chance—perhaps his only chance at slowing down Gorman—would be to fire blindly out the window, emptying both Colts if necessary before going to the rifle. He checked the cylinder on Buttermilk's Colt. It was fully loaded.

A movement off to his left caught his eye. Upon closer scrutiny, he determined that it was neither man nor horse—but smoke. It came from behind the barn. His immediate impression was that the barn or the adjoining tack room might be on fire, but such a move made no sense to him. Firing the ranch house, however, made more sense. He guessed that he must be seeing smoke from a torch. Of course, the barn and the tack room would provide cover for them, enabling them to get within seventy or eighty feet of the house. Hawthorne gauged distances and angles and took up a position as close to the opening of the window as he could without exposing himself.

Hawthorne spotted movement—a rifle among some rocks beyond the corrals, and he knew the next barrage was about to begin. He knelt down beneath the window. Seconds later the firing started. He raised the Colts just enough to clear the window sill. As quickly as he could, he loosed all twelve rounds at the spot where he suspected that a man with a torch would be making his way toward the ranch house.

The barrage stopped; this time it did not last as long.

Hawthorne dropped the Colts, picked up the rifle, and stood at the side of the window. He chanced a peek. A man lay on the ground, his arms and legs twisted at an awkward angle. A torch lay beside him, guttering in the dirt.

Hawthorne considered that they might try it again, but he doubted it, at least not in the same way. He rested the rifle against the wall and began to reload the Colts, all the while keeping his eyes on the area in front of the ranch house. Far to the east, well beyond the barn, stretched a scattering of boulders. They would provide adequate cover for Gorman's men should they choose to approach from that side, and five minutes later, that was exactly what they did. Hawthorne could see two men making for the boulders. It would take them longer, but they would no doubt find the ranch house more accessible from that direction, where Hawthorne and the others would be blindsided. Since there were no windows on the east wall, Hawthorne could do virtually nothing to prevent their attack.

Hawthorne heard a low moaning sound. He turned to see Buttermilk lying on his side, his head cradled on Lane's lap. His eyes looked glassy, his face drained. His lips moved but no words came out. Finally, he managed to speak. "I'm sorry, Trace. I'm sorry I got you into this mess. I'm sorry for you too, Mr. Malverne."

Malverne stared at him, obviously confused by his words.

"What do you mean, Uncle Cal? This isn't your fault."

"I'm afraid it is, girl. I'm the one who set those buzzards on us."

Lane looked at him in shock.

"That's right, child. I did it, and I did wrong." He coughed as his hand moved slowly to his chest.

Lane's eyes were wide, her face revealing her inner

turmoil as she looked from Buttermilk to Hawthorne. "What does he mean, Marshal?"

Hawthorne swallowed hard. "We can talk about it later, when we're safe," he said, turning his attention once again to the outside.

"But I don't understand. I—"

Hawthorne held up his hand for silence.

There was a sound outside, followed by a loud noise like something striking the roof.

Malverne rose to his feet and stared at the ceiling.

"What is it?" Lane asked.

"I think they've torched the house," Hawthorne said.

"But the house is made of stone," Lane pointed out, an edge of desperation in her voice.

"Yes, but the roof isn't."

Within minutes, they could hear crackling. The sound was followed by a thin wisp of smoke penetrating the beams overhead.

"What can we do?" Malverne asked.

"The smoke will rise. If we stay low to the floor, we should be all right for a while," Hawthorne replied. "At least they won't rush us now. There's no point to it. They've got us right where they want us."

"Then what?"

Hawthorne cast a glance at the ceiling. "When the beams get too weak, the roof will collapse."

Malverne shook his head. "Then it's either dying from the smoke or being crushed under the roof."

Hawthorne nodded.

"Can't we make a break for it?"

"They're out there waiting for us to do just that. We'd have to cross at least seventy feet of open ground to reach any cover. They'd cut us down like cornstalks. Besides, all the horses have been scattered. There would be nowhere to go."

Malverne stared at the smoke curling around the beams overhead. "I didn't count on dying like this. I say we make a run for the rocks . . . anywhere."

"What about Buttermilk? Do we carry him?"

Malverne considered Buttermilk, whose eyes were closed tight, a pained expression on his face as he was laboring to breathe.

Lane fixed pleading eyes on Malverne. "I can't leave him." She paused for thought, frowning, pursing her lips. "But if you want to try to get away, go ahead. I'll understand, but I can't go without him."

Malverne shook his head in resignation. "No, it isn't right that you should have to leave him. I suppose dying one way is as good as another," he said as he slumped down next to Buttermilk.

Hawthorne decided that there was something about Malverne that he liked.

It did not take long for the smoke to worsen. The ranch house was being engulfed in it, and everyone was coughing. Malverne and Lane doused some cloths and draped them over their heads. They placed one over Buttermilk and gave one to Hawthorne. They helped some. Ashes and sparks showered them, and when one of the overhead beams threatened to give way, they were forced to move Buttermilk to another part of the room. As they carried him, he began to cough badly and pulled the cloth from his face. He opened his eyes and managed to focus on Hawthorne.

"Trace."

"How're you doing, Cal?"

"Can't complain."

"Try to hold on, partner . . . until I can figure a way for us to get out of here."

"Trace, I never trusted those boys from the beginnin', and when you told me what that telegram meant . . . well, I decided to give us some insurance."

Hawthorne knelt beside him, placing his ear next to Buttermilk's lips, for the old man was weak, and his faltering words were barely audible.

"When I was buildin' this house, there were some renegade Shoshones on the loose. I was afraid of bein' trapped inside just as we are now." He coughed, a rasping cough from deep within his chest. "You know . . . 'afore I started bustin' wild oaters for a livin', I did some prospectin'. There's an old mine behind us. I spent months in it prior to workin' at my present trade. I got nothin' out of it but fool's gold and calluses. The shaft runs halfway through the mountain and out to daylight behind some thick brush on the west side. 'Afore supper, I put four fresh horses near the opening of the shaft. Looks like you'll be needin' only three."

Hawthorne patted Buttermilk on the shoulder.

"The china cabinet. Move it aside. That's your way out, boy."

Hawthorne stared at Buttermilk in disbelief.

"Take care of Lane." His eyes started to close.

Quickly, Hawthorne got to his feet and moved to the cabinet. He stood beside it and pushed. It was a large, heavy piece of furniture, and it did not budge. He crouched lower, put his shoulder against the wood, and shoved it with all he had. Grudgingly, it trembled and he could see the base move slightly. He coughed as the smoke swirled around him, now making it difficult even to see the others across the room. Hawthorne steadied himself, bent lower to the floor, and threw all his weight against the cabinet. This time it moved across the floor—an inch at first, then another, until Hawthorne had pushed the cabinet nearly two feet away from its original position. He stepped back from the wall and faced a gaping black hole covered with cobwebs, as the stale air was sucked out by the fire in the ceiling.

Hawthorne picked up a kerosene lamp, lit it, and took a few steps into the shaft, brushing away webs as he moved. The walls were dark, and the undisturbed layers of dirt on the floor told him that no one had trod here in many a year. He checked the shoring. Old as the timbers must have been, they seemed adequate. He set the lamp on a rock and returned to the house.

Lane's head was resting on Buttermilk's chest. Malverne was lying on the floor, his head still covered with the cloth. Smoke was gutting the house now, grayish-black in color, making it hard to breathe. Hawthorne's eyes widened as he stepped across the room and called to the others. At first, they did not respond. He nudged Malverne's shoulder. Malverne stirred slightly but did not get up. Hawthorne shook him more vigorously and helped him to sit. Lane was coughing. Hawthorne picked her up and carried her into the shaft. He placed her next to the lamp and returned to the house. Malverne was still sitting, dazed, coughing. Hawthorne regarded Buttermilk closely. He shook his head sadly and then grabbed a coverlet off one of the chairs and placed it over Buttermilk's face. Gently, he lifted Buttermilk off the floor.

"He's gone, Marshal," Malverne managed to say.

"I know. I just don't want to see his body destroyed like this in a heap of ashes."

Malverne stumbled to his feet and blindly followed Hawthorne into the shaft, which was rapidly being filled with smoke.

Lane was sitting up, clearing her throat and rubbing her eyes. She watched as Hawthorne tenderly placed Buttermilk's body beside her.

"He's dead, Lane."

She nodded. "I know."

"We have to leave him here for now. We have to move quickly. I promise to return later to see that he gets a proper burial."

Lane lowered her head as she brushed tears from her cheeks.

Hawthorne rose to his feet and turned back toward the ranch house.

"Where are you going?" Malverne asked.

"I want to close the entrance to this shaft again. If the cabinet doesn't completely burn, they may not know exactly how we got out. No sense in drawing them a map, and it may buy us some time."

He moved hurriedly through the gathering smoke. When he reached the ranch house, he could see flames licking the beams in the ceiling. The supports were charred and uncertain. He removed his bandanna and fashioned it around his nose and mouth. Keeping low to the floor, he made his way into the kitchen, where he grabbed a few articles and stuffed them into a sack. On his way out, he lifted a pair of hats from a wall hook and then made a hasty retreat into the mine shaft. He struggled to replace the cabinet in its original position and then returned to Malverne and Lane. He got them on their feet, hoisted the lamp, and led the way down the shaft. It was an easy walk. The shaft ran straight into the mountain for about one hundred feet before angling to the left. A short distance ahead revealed a meager ray of light. As they approached it, they could hear the soft nickering of a horse. Hawthorne extinguished the lamp and set it down. Another twenty feet brought them to a large cavern. As Buttermilk had stated, four horses were secured to a rope which ran the length of the chamber. Saddles, blankets, and bridles were neatly deposited nearby. The entrance to the cavern was concealed by thick brush which allowed enough light to indicate a way of passage and served to guard against any unwanted intruder.

With Malverne and Lane assisting as much as possible, Hawthorne proceeded to saddle the horses. They were fresh and sturdy. Knowing Hawthorne's needs, Buttermilk had obviously selected the best mounts he had available. Hawthorne secured the food sack onto the saddle horn of one of the horses, which he would use as a backup. After seeing Lane help Malverne mount, then get aboard, he tightened the cinch on the last horse and swung into the saddle. He led the way out of the cavern, through the brush, and down a winding, forgotten trail that bordered the mountain on the west.

Chapter Seven

Hawthorne stood on a rocky knoll and scanned the horizon behind him. He could see a black plume of smoke rising slowly into the sky. It marred a ceiling of blue that was perfect save for a smattering of drifting cirrus clouds. He was saddened by the sight, for he knew that it marked the end of an era for him. He had always held Buttermilk in high regard, and despite the fact that the old-timer had given him up for money, Hawthorne knew that nothing would alter the good memories he had of a man he admired. It was a bad way to die, bushwhacked . . . backshot on your own spread, your homestead burned to the ground around you. It was no way for anyone to die—another shattered life, another notch in an endless series of notches carved by Max McCargo.

Hawthorne stepped down from his vantage point and descended into a small ravine where Malverne and

Lane were resting. There was a trickle of runoff water from somewhere deep within the rocks that gathered into a small pool. The horses had been watered and the canteens had been filled.

"Any sign of them?" Malverne asked, his face drawn, his good arm cradling the one he carried in a sling.

"None, but it will only be a matter of time before they discover we're not in the ranch house."

"Then they'll follow."

"Yes."

"How much of a start do you think we have on them?"

"It's hard to tell. It depends on how quickly they pick up our trail. I'd say we're three, maybe four hours ahead of them."

"That's not much."

"No, but there isn't more than an hour and a half of daylight left. They won't be able to track us in the dark, and we'll keep moving, through a good portion of the night. With any luck, we'll at least double our lead."

"But what's the difference? They know where we're going. Besides, there have to be plenty more of them between here and Grand City. They're probably just lying in wait."

Hawthorne smiled. "Drink as much as possible now. There won't be any water where we're going—not for at least two days," he said as he dipped his bandanna into the water and mopped his face and neck with it.

"You're not thinking of crossing the desert, are you?" Malverne asked, deep concern lining his face.

"I'm afraid so. I would've preferred to have packed extra canteens, but under the circumstances, we're lucky to have gotten away with our skins."

"But there's nothing out there—no shade, no grass— nothing but waste for days on end. We'd never make it. Especially not a woman."

Hawthorne glanced at Lane, who had been sitting by quietly, listening.

"Don't worry about me," she said. "Do what you have to."

"But if we head into the desert, we'd be going west. Grand City is north."

"We're not going to Grand City," Hawthorne announced as he rolled his bandanna and replaced it around his neck.

Malverne eyed him uncertainly. "What do you mean? What about the trial?"

"The governor knows that McCargo has a small army out looking for us. That's my concern. He also knows that Grand City will be surrounded by McCargo's guns. That's where he was able to help us."

"How's that?"

"By arranging for a change of venue. McCargo will be tried in Cairo Wells."

"Cairo Wells? That's in the middle of nowhere. It's in the desert," Malverne said, somewhat surprised at Hawthorne's news.

"It's on the fringe of it anyway. With luck, we

should be there a full day before McCargo even learns about it. By then, we can have you holed up before McCargo's wolves can close in. That means we have a chance, a good one, of getting you to trial."

Malverne digested this unexpected bit of information. Somehow it made good sense, and for the first time he felt they could reach their destination.

As Hawthorne double-checked the horses, he assessed their situation. He had his rifle and ammunition. Buttermilk had left his primary gear in the shaft. Their horses were fresh. They were well equipped with everything except food and water. He had managed to snatch some beans, bacon, and cornbread from the kitchen. Along with some jerked beef he had in his saddlebags, it would last them for a while. The water was more of a problem. He would have to gamble on their having enough until they reached the next water hole. Alone, he knew he could make it, but his principal concern lay with Lane. Malverne was right. It would not be an easy trip for her, yet there was nowhere else he could take her. She had to come along and play out the hand with them.

They all mounted, each alone with his or her own thoughts as Hawthorne led the way down the ravine past a deposit of shattered boulders onto softer sand that was dotted with sage and occasional pecks of scrub cedar. Hawthorne led the spare mount, Lane followed, and Malverne trailed behind. They rode in silence, the only sounds being the muffled tread of the horses' hooves on the painted sand. In time, the moon sat in the sky, bathing the desert in a soft glow that offered some security in the alien landscape.

Charles Blake stood in front of his office window and watched people move up and down the main street of Grand City. He wondered what kinds of problems each of them had. The cattleman was most likely concerned with getting a fair price for his beef. The farmer was worried about bringing in a crop or making a mortgage payment. The shopkeeper was intent on improving his line of merchandise. The one thing shared by all of them seemed to be problems. Blake considered himself to be no exception. His problems were not unique, but they did seem insurmountable.

A barely audible knock broke his train of thought. He turned, watched his door open slowly, and saw Myra Fontaine slip into the room. She closed the door behind her and stood with her back to it as though in fear. She was stunning. She wore a forest-green dress with large black buttons and a matching hat with a cluster of feathers. She carried a parasol and a string purse.

"I hope you didn't mind my coming like this," she said.

Blake was a bit surprised, for she had never before visited his office. "No," he managed to say, "but do you think it's wise? I mean . . . I'm sure he's having both of us watched."

"He is. Brill Cotton has been keeping tabs on me. I had a couple of the chorus girls distract him long

enough for me to cross the street and sneak into your
office the back way."

"My secretary . . . she—"

"Surely, you can trust her?"

"I . . . well . . . yes, of course I can."

"Besides, I think she knows—I mean about us."

"How could she? I've never even discussed you
with her."

"It was the way she looked at me when I walked in
and asked to see you. A woman can tell those things."

Blake nodded his understanding. "Yes, I suppose a
woman can."

Myra did not reply.

Blake felt uneasy. "Would you like a drink?"

"No."

"What is it? I mean, why did you come here? Is
there anything wrong?"

"No, I just wondered if you had heard any news
about Malverne."

"No. There's been nothing."

"I see," she said, lowering her head. Then, after a
pause she added, "Maybe that's a good sign."

"Maybe."

"Have you thought any more about . . . about what
we discussed the other night?" Her eyes were intense,
almost desperate. Her voice was cracking.

"I've thought about nothing else, but—"

"Yes?"

"But frankly, I don't think that we stand much of a
chance."

"If there's any chance at all, I'd be willing to take it . . . as long as I'm with you."

Blake regarded her closely. He knew from her eyes, from the desperation and sincerity in her voice that her heart was speaking for her. He crossed the room, put his arms around her, and kissed her long and full. When their lips parted, they opened their eyes and looked at each other. Blake pulled her to him again, more tightly, and kissed her. He could feel the delicate ridge of her spine and her heart beating quickly against his chest. She seemed so fragile, so breakable in his arms, quite the contrast from the outgoing stage performer whose glamorous presence lent so much to her reputation as a star attraction throughout the country. She was vulnerable, timid. He knew he loved her. He had loved her from the beginning, and he wanted to protect her, yet he was also astute enough to comprehend the reality of their situation.

As he drew away from her, he knew he would disappoint her with his response, but he also knew that to deceive her by offering her any false hopes would be cruel.

"I don't like what's going on any more than you do. I can see that we're both being torn apart, but Mr. McCargo has an army at his disposal. I can't even use a gun." He waved his hand at his shelves of law books. "These are my tools. What could I do against such odds? Out here on the frontier I'm just not much of a man."

Myra wrung her hands as she listened to his words, words she expected to hear but had hoped she would not. "You're a man, Charles, a good one. In fact, you don't give yourself enough credit. There aren't many men I know who could have lasted as long as you have dealing with a creature like Max McCargo. But I understand."

He turned and took a step toward her. "It's just that—"

"You don't have to explain," she said. "You don't owe me an explanation. The bottom line is that I'm in love with you. I want to be able to walk down the street with you, with my arm in yours. I can't do that in Grand City, and I can't do it at all as long as Max McCargo has such a stranglehold on our lives. Perhaps we'll meet again some day in another place when all of this is behind us."

"Meet again? What do you mean? What are you going to do?" Blake asked in surprise.

She shrugged her shoulders. "I don't know exactly, but I'm going to run as far and as fast as I can. I'll do anything to get away from here and Max Mc-Cargo."

"He'll find you."

"He might, but I'll run away again and keep running."

Myra stared at him as though she expected him to say something.

Blake considered her words, contemplating what he should say or do.

Finally, Myra smiled and said, "Good-bye, Charles. Good luck."

She turned and walked to the door. As she placed

her hand on the knob, she paused. She looked down and saw Blake's hand on her arm.

"I've been working on a plan," he announced hesitantly. "It's not likely that it will work, but if we go down, we might as well go down together."

Chapter Eight

Hawthorne stopped about four hours before day-break. He decided to make camp in a dry wash that formed a bowl. He dismounted and then hobbled his horse and the spare. Malverne followed suit. Lane, distraught and overcome with fatigue, had to be helped from her horse. She was shivering and nearly fell into Hawthorne's arms as he led her to a soft bank of sand. Malverne broke out the bedrolls while Hawthorne gathered some sticks. In a few minutes, he had a fire going, which provided them all with the warmth they needed to counter the drop in temperature in the desert at night. Malverne sat close to the fire and warmed his hands, still moving somewhat awkwardly with the sling around his arm. In a matter of minutes, he turned onto his side and fell asleep. Lane sat up, her arms wrapped around her legs as she drew her knees up to her chin. She sat there shivering, staring morosely into the flames.

Hawthorne sat down beside her and wrapped a blanket around her shoulders. "Are you all right, Lane?" he asked.

She nodded her head without taking her eyes off the flames, which cast strange shadows in the wash as they circled and danced around the sticks.

"Still cold?"

"A little."

"The fire will cure that in a while."

Slowly, her eyes left the fire and focused on him. "Marshal, before Uncle Cal died, he said that all of this was his fault. What did he mean?"

Hawthorne considered how he could go about answering her question without causing her any more pain. He did not know exactly how to do it, and he began groping for the right words when Lane interrupted his thoughts.

"Tell me, Marshal. I want to know. I have to know."

He looked into her eyes and saw someone who was older than her years. He knew that she meant what she said, and at that moment he also knew that the straight truth was in order, and he told it.

Lane listened, her eyes never leaving his face as he explained Buttermilk's role in the assault on the ranch house. When he finished, he saw tears form in Lane's eyes.

"Oh, Marshal, I'm so ashamed of what Uncle Cal did. It was wrong, no matter what the reason."

"Yes, it was, but I'm not ashamed of him."

She regarded him closely.

"I knew your uncle for the better part of my life. He was always an honest, decent man. What he did might have been wrong, but he did it because he loved you . . . and remember, he did try to set things right, only it was too late. Sure, it was a mistake, but even a good man makes mistakes. Your uncle was a good man. Try to remember him as he was. I'm going to."

In a while, the tears dried up in Lane's eyes and she managed a smile. She put her arms around Hawthorne's neck and hugged him tightly. He held her for a moment, and a strange sensation came over him, a warm feeling the likes of which he had never felt before . . . at least not in this fashion.

"I'm tired, Marshal," she whispered in his ear.

He helped her into her bedroll and covered her with the extra blanket. In a minute her eyes closed, and Hawthorne found himself sitting alone by the fire, his thoughts centering on Lane Carter as well as Malverne, the trial, and the men who were following them.

Mace Gorman sat atop his paint, his right leg curled nonchalantly around his saddle horn. He took a long swallow from his canteen, swished it through his teeth, and spat it out on the sand. He watched as Avery Truman and Burr Denton rode up.

"They're headed out into the desert all right . . . four horses," Truman announced.

"How much of a start?"

Truman reassessed the ground. "Six, maybe eight hours. They must've traveled during the night."

"Yeah, but why west?" Denton asked. "They're not headed anywhere near Grand City."

"That's a good question. I've been wonderin' about that myself," Gorman replied.

"Maybe it's just a trick to draw us off. They might be plannin' on changin' direction once they're out in the middle of nowhere," Denton offered.

"Could be, but what's the point? We know where they're headed. Who they aimin' to fool?" Truman added.

Denton scratched the stubble on his chin and spat a brown stream of tobacco juice, a muddled expression on his craggy face.

"Four horses, you say?" Gorman asked.

"That's right. Judgin' from the tracks, one of 'em is a spare," Denton announced.

"One of 'em would be Malverne," Gorman said. "The second would most likely be the old man's niece—the one he told me he wanted protected. The third one must be that lawdog the old man mentioned. Just who do you figure he is?"

Truman and Denton looked at each other.

"We've been mullin' that over," Truman said. "There's a U.S. marshal I once saw at Spencer—name of Hawthorne. This hombre who shot it out with us at the ranch house looks a lot like him."

"Yeah, I heard tell of him, and the way he handled those Colts . . . there can't be two of 'em," Denton said.

A slow smile crept over Gorman's face. "Hawthorne . . . yeah, I know the name. Never had the pleasure, but Mr. McCargo was some put out because of him a few times. I was wonderin' when the two of us were goin' to cross trails. Looks like it's about that time."

"Sounds like you're aimin' to make this personal, Gorman," Truman said, eying the big man warily.

Gorman's eyes landed on Truman, who withered under their coldness.

"Our job is to make sure they don't reach Grand City in time for the trial. If we can force 'em out into the desert, we can guarantee they won't make it. On top of that, Mr. McCargo wants Malverne's head, and for $20,000, I'll follow the devil himself into Hades to bring it back."

Truman and Denton glanced at each other. Neither was anxious to cross the desert, but neither was willing to defy Gorman's orders either.

Denton cast his eyes over the tract of wasteland. "I've known a few boys who ventured out there. Most of 'em didn't come back. Those that did were never right in the head again."

"They're out there. If they don't make it, we'll find their bones. If they do make it, we sure enough can. Besides, how far can a woman travel in this inferno? Even with the lead they have on us, we should be able to overtake 'em in a few days," Gorman stated.

Truman and Denton knew it was futile to argue with Gorman. They remained silent as they watched him stare at the horizon, which was blurred by heatwaves and the glare of the sun.

Finally, Gorman said, "Get the boys. We'll start right away."

Every Wednesday afternoon since she had been in Grand City, Myra rented a rig from Hadley's livery stable and drove out into the countryside. It was her getaway time, an occasion when she could escape the activity of Grand City and be alone in a quiet glade by a small waterfall. She usually spent an hour or so sitting and thinking before she drove back. Sometimes she would pack a light lunch. This Wednesday was like any other. She wore a loose-fitting blouse, pants, boots, and a Stetson, but she filled her basket with extra food. She rode out of town at the same time, at the same pace, and made her way to her favorite spot—exactly as Blake had instructed.

Blake, in the meantime, following his daily visit to Max McCargo's cell, ran a series of errands which included the post office, the telegraph, and the bank before returning to his office. He greeted Mrs. Harker as he entered and told her he was not to be disturbed until after lunch. He then locked his office door, changed into some trail clothes, and stepped through his rear door to an alleyway which accessed his office building. There were two saddled horses at the hitching post waiting for him. Casting furtive glances about him, he mounted one of the horses and led the other through the alley, past the rear of the druggist and the optician, where he paused for several minutes, watching and waiting. When he was absolutely certain no one was in the vicinity, he quickly crossed over a small side street into another alley. A series of twists and turns past fences and through gates led him to the outskirts of town. He forsook the main road for a back trail that disappeared into the tree line where he was soon swallowed up by pinon pines and cedars.

In twenty minutes he found Myra, standing anxiously beside her rig in a tiny clearing. She smiled nervously when she saw him approach, and when he dismounted, she threw her arms around him, partly out of fear and partly at the joy of seeing him.

"Did everything go as planned?" she asked tensely.

"Yes," he said, taking a deep breath. "I don't know how I followed through with everything without betraying myself. Maybe I didn't."

"I'm sure you were just fine," she said, looking up at him proudly.

"You know, it's a funny thing, I always considered myself a pretty cool customer in a courtroom, but I can tell you . . . back there in town my knees were none too steady."

"That's quite a coincidence because I always looked upon myself as a consummate performer when I played to full houses, but I do believe I had a bit of stage fright this morning."

The two of them laughed at their situation. Then, their smiles dissolved as they stared into each other's eyes, and their lips met again.

"We'd better get moving if we want to catch that stage," Blake said as he pulled away from her.

She nodded.

Blake stored the food that Myra brought into the

saddlebags and helped her mount the second horse. Then, for the next two hours they rode steadily, with little conversation, intent on putting as much distance as possible between Grand City and themselves.

Myra watched Blake as he sat in the grass, eating the chicken and biscuits that she had packed. He ate hungrily, without speaking, his eyes focused on some invisible object at his feet, his thoughts obviously far away.

"Are you all right, Charles?" she finally asked, uncomfortable with his silence.

He nodded as he wiped his mouth with a napkin.

"You haven't spoken a word for ten minutes," she said.

"I'm sorry. I was just thinking."

"Are you still worried?"

"Yes."

"Talk to me about it," she urged.

He swallowed a last bite of biscuit and then wiped his hands. "I know that Brill Cotton was watching me today as I made my way about town. It was subtle but at the same time obvious. I laid a false trail for his benefit."

"What do you mean?"

"I withdrew some money from my bank account and wired it to the postmaster in Silver Mesa—to be held until called for by C. Baker."

"And who is C. Baker?"

"There is no C. Baker. I'm depending on Brill Cotton to check the wire I sent. He's already suspicious.

I'm hoping he sees the similarity between the initials of my name and those in the name C. Baker. It's a thinly veiled disguise, simple enough for someone like Brill Cotton to penetrate. When he discovers I've skipped town, it might make him think I'm going to Silver Mesa to pick up that money, which happens to be in the opposite direction from the one we're going."

"That was clever."

"Maybe, but right about now I'd rather have that cash in hand. I only had about a thousand in my office safe. That won't last us very long."

"I have nearly seven hundred. Between the two of us, we should be all right."

He shrugged dubiously. "We have a long way to go. We need money for the stage and the train. Accommodations are expensive. We'll need food, additional clothes, and the like."

"We'll get by. If we're together, we'll make it," Myra said reassuringly.

"I'll have to change my name. You might not be able to perform for a while anyway."

"You explained all that before. I'm willing to make that sacrifice."

All at once, Blake froze.

"What is it?" Myra asked, stunned by the sudden change that came over him.

"Did you hear something?" he asked as he climbed to his feet.

"No. What is it?" she asked, looking around anxiously.

"I don't know." He walked to the brush nearby and entered it cautiously.

"Be careful, Charles," Myra warned.

In a moment he emerged. He strolled over to the horses, patted them down, and then returned to Myra's side. "I guess I'm just a little spooked. I thought I heard something. It was probably a rabbit."

Myra started to breathe again, not realizing for a moment that she had stopped. "Charles, I hope I haven't slowed us up too much. I know I don't ride all that well."

"You're doing fine, Myra." He pulled out his pocket watch, studied it, and clicked it shut. "In fact, we're ahead of schedule." He sat down again next to her. "Once the stage gets us to Lordsburg, we'll be out of the county. That's our first step. Then, the train will get us out of the state. Maybe when we reach St. Louis, we can lose ourselves, lie low for a while. Then, we'll head back East."

"Where you go, I go. No matter what happens, I want to be with you."

Blake regarded her closely. He reached over, took her hand in his hands, and kissed her gently. He kissed her again, more fully, and then pulled her down in the grass beside him and wrapped her in his arms.

Chapter Nine

Blake cursed when the stationmaster told him that
the stage would be an hour late. Myra clutched his
hand, and he regained his composure. He took advantage of the time, however, to sell their horses and saddles to the stage line for a fair price. He and Myra
then sat on one of the benches on the front porch and
discussed their situation.

"So far so good," he announced. "We made it this
far without interference, but I'll feel a lot better once
we get on board that stage and get moving."

"They could still catch up with us, couldn't they?"

"They could, but every mile we cover increases the
odds in our favor . . . and every hour we sit here places
us in just that much more jeopardy."

Myra moved closer to him and rested her head on
his shoulder.

"Tired?" he asked, as he looked down at her.

"A little. More scared, I'd say."

"Yeah, me too. You know, it's kind of amusing. Here we are, running away like a couple of bank robbers, looking over our shoulders, jumping at shadows. I guess people just wouldn't understand."

"They would if they knew Max McCargo the way we do."

"How did you ever come to get mixed up with him anyway?"

Blake leaned back, stared at the clouds, and reflected. "It was a long time ago . . . about eight years. I came west for new opportunities, a chance to use my law degree to help better mankind." He smiled. "In one of my earlier cases, I defended a farmer. I can't even remember the details of the trial, but I won the case. The man who brought charges against the farmer was Max McCargo. He was impressed with me, took me to dinner, struck up a friendship. A month or so later he hired me to represent him over a land dispute. I did. I won the case, and he was very grateful. One thing led to another, and before long he retained me at an impressive yearly salary. But from that point on, I lost my soul. What I didn't know at the time was that I had penned a covenant with the devil himself. Oh, things went fine for some time. In fact, I believed in Mr. McCargo. I considered him to be a great man. I trusted him despite stories, rumors. In time, however, I came to learn exactly what he was—a liar, a thief, a land grabber, and a killer. He used the law and me to his advantage. The wealthier and more powerful he became, the more cautious he was from a legal standpoint. I kept everything legal, you understand, at least on the surface. That was my job, and I did it well. I could keep things legal, but I couldn't make them right. By the time I discovered what Mr. McCargo really was, I was in too deep. I had allowed myself to be manipulated. I had become the principal legal instrument of the biggest criminal in the state. Nevertheless, I stayed on. The money was good; I had connections, both social and financial. I had clothes, a fine office. Then, Mr. McCargo began making demands of me that exceeded my legal scope and my loyalty to him. There were orders to have people hurt, to have their land taken away. Early on, the money kept me. Then it was fear."

"I know about that," Myra put in.

"I'm sure you do. I actually reached the point where I feared for my own safety to say no to Max Mc-Cargo."

"You couldn't go to the law?"

"There are few lawmen who aren't in Mr. Mc-Cargo's pocket. Most of those who are honest fear him or can do little or nothing against his machine."

"It's hard to believe that there's no one who can stop him."

Blake looked into her eyes. "I didn't say he couldn't be stopped, and I didn't say there weren't men capable of stopping him."

"What men?"

"Well, the governor, for one. He's managed to do pretty well against Mr. McCargo. In fact, he has enough evidence to hang him twice over; that is, if Malverne ever gets to give testimony."

"And who else, besides the governor?"

"There's a U.S. marshal named Trace Hawthorne. I don't know much about him, but I do know that he doesn't scare. Mr. McCargo has had some run-ins with Hawthorne before, and it pleases me to say that Mr. McCargo came out on the short end."

"Do you think this Marshal Hawthorne has something to do with the governor's case?" Myra asked.

"I wouldn't be surprised," he said, smiling.

The stage was an hour and a half late. The spent horses were changed for fresh ones while the driver had something to eat.

Blake and Myra boarded the stage and sat alone inside. They held each other's hand as they waited somewhat impatiently to be under way.

"At least we'll have the coach to ourselves," Myra announced, smiling at Blake.

Suddenly, the door opened, and Blake and Myra saw a shadow pass over the floor.

"You won't be needin' your tickets this trip, lawyer, and the two of you won't be alone either," Brill Cotton announced as he stuck his head in the coach, flashing an irregular row of stained teeth beneath his rank mustache.

Myra huddled next to Blake as they sat in front of a campfire.

Cotton sat opposite them, finishing his plate of pork rinds. He ate greedily, with little regard for manners as he licked his plate upon completion and wiped his mouth on his shirtsleeve. He then picked up his coffee cup and blew into it several times before sipping the steaming brew.

"Yes, sir, you sure did somethin' mighty bad to rile Mr. McCargo the way you did, lawyer man—aside that is, from runnin' off with his woman," Cotton proclaimed.

The comment piqued Blake's attention. "Exactly what are you talking about, Cotton?"

"Well, I don't exactly know, but there was a telegram sent over to the jailhouse early this afternoon that nearly set fire to the boss. I don't know what was in it, but I did catch wind of one word—Jimson."

The name hit Blake hard, so much so that Myra felt him stiffen next to her.

"What is it? Who's Jimson?" Myra whispered into Blake's ear.

"He's our informant in the governor's office. I don't know his real name; he just goes by Jimson. He's been working with Mr. McCargo, feeding him information in an effort to undermine the governor's investigation. I think the governor has been onto him for some time though. The telegram could mean one of two things. It could mean that Jimson alerted Mr. McCargo that he's been found out, or . . ."

"Or what?"

Blake considered the matter for a long moment. "Since the telegram provoked Mr. McCargo into siccing Cotton on me so suddenly, more than likely it means that I'm the one who has been discovered."

"What do you mean?"

Blake's eyes locked onto Myra's. He studied her features in the light of the campfire. He secretly wished that he could have met her a long time ago. "When you were a child, did you ever go to a circus?"

"Yes, of course," she replied, a bit puzzled by his question.

"Did you ever see the tightrope walker?"

She nodded.

"Well, for quite a while now I've been walking a tightrope. Today, I'm afraid that I've finally fallen off."

She stared at him.

"What I'm trying to tell you is that for some time I've been secretly working with the governor, giving him as much information as I could about Mr. Mc-Cargo. It's been a touchy situation, you understand. Mr. McCargo is still my client. What he tells me is privileged information, and as his attorney, I've never violated that information. Believe me, if I could testify against him in a court of law, I would. I can't, but someone like Malverne could. However, there were occasions when I became aware of some of Mr. McCargo's plans. I learned about attacks on people, raids, threats, and the like. Sometimes I wasn't in a position to be able to do anything about them without painting myself into a corner. But there were times when I was able to do some good . . . to prevent a barn from being torched or to save a man from a beating."

Myra wrapped her arm through Blake's tightly.

"I wasn't able to do much. Maybe I just did it to ease a guilty conscience."

"I think you're wonderful, and I believe that you're a far more courageous man than you realize."

He shrugged. "I don't feel so courageous right now. If Mr. McCargo found out about me . . . well, I'm surprised he hasn't had Cotton just do away with me and leave me out here for the buzzards."

"That isn't Max McCargo's way though, is it?"

"No, it isn't. I'm sure he'd take great pleasure in thinking of something far more disagreeable."

"Why don't the both of you stop your jawin', and you, Miss Myra, get me some more coffee," Cotton ordered, as he turned over his empty cup.

"What kind of talk is that? Miss Fontaine is not your servant."

Cotton grinned. "You know, I've got a notion that Mr. McCargo has got somethin' special planned for you, lawyer man. But Mr. McCargo says that me and the boys can have Miss Myra here. So now's as good a time as any for her to start gettin' in the practice of bein' hospitable."

Myra flinched at the remark.

"Get the coffee yourself, Cotton," Blake said.

Cotton smirked. "You know, Blake, Mr. McCargo ain't too concerned about what condition you're in when I bring you back—as long as you're alive. If you prove to be too much of a burr under my saddle blanket, I'll be glad to show you how good I am with a pistol barrel."

"Please, Blake," Myra intervened.

"Tell me, Cotton. Just how did you manage to find us so quickly? I thought I covered my trail reasonably well," Blake asked, attempting to defuse Cotton's sudden urge for violence.

"It was Jimmy Seavers who set me on to your notion," Cotton boasted smugly.

"Jimmy? The stablehand?"

"That's right. He told me all about the horses he saddled and left just for you."

"I don't believe it. Jimmy wouldn't talk."

"Oh, he didn't mean to, but you'd be surprised to see how talkative he got once his front teeth were knocked out." Cotton laughed out loud.

"That boy was just fifteen years old," Blake whispered to Myra in disgust.

Cotton rattled his tin cup on a rock. "I'm waitin', Myra. I could use a little more coffee. It's goin' to be a cold night."

"As I said, Cotton, get the coffee yourself."

Cotton started to climb to his feet, but Myra jumped up quickly.

"I'll get your coffee," she said, moving hastily to the fire.

"That's more like it," Cotton returned, sitting down again and stretching out his legs. "Fill it to the rim and have some yourself. There's plenty to go around."

Blake was seething inside, outraged by Cotton's impertinence.

Myra's hands were trembling as she neared Cotton, who eyed her lustily. She filled his cup as he requested, and he took a sip, the steam escaping around his mustache. Myra glanced at Blake, who was watching the scene uneasily. She turned, hesitated, opened the lid of the coffeepot, and then dumped the contents between Cotton's legs.

Cotton dropped his cup. He opened his mouth, but for a moment, no sound came out. Then, he emitted a wail that might have been heard for a mile through the trees. Cotton clutched his crotch and rolled over onto the dirt.

In an instant, Blake was on his feet. He rushed to Cotton's side and removed the gun from his holster.

"Ahhhh! I'm burning up! You burned me, you dirty—"

Cotton's words ended with a sharp intake of breath as Blake kicked him in the ribs.

"That's for Jimmy!" Blake declared.

"Oh, Charles," Myra cried out.

Blake turned. He saw Myra standing near the fire, shaking violently. She let the coffeepot drop to the ground and lifted her hands to her face. He moved to her side and put his arms around her. "It's all right. He won't bother us any more."

"What do we do now?" she asked.

"Well, one thing's certain. We can't go back to Grand City. And we're not going to run anymore. Since there doesn't seem to be any reason to keep any secrets any longer, we might as well lay our cards on the table. I'll contact the governor. He can give us protection. We'll let him make the call."

Chapter Ten

The heat was intense. The glare of the sun was relentless. A barren, unimaginative, ruthless arena spread before them as they trudged along. Heat waves danced in the distance like a floating lake. There was a sullen loneliness about the sea of sand, which seemed to stretch on as far as the eye could see. Malverne felt it. Lane sensed it. Only Hawthorne was unaffected, for he was no stranger to loneliness and isolation. He alone could exist in such wasteland. In fact, he could thrive here, for he knew and respected the land. Whereas it offered emptiness and desolation to most, it had once given him hope and security.

Following a meager breakfast, the trio of travellers pushed on. There would be no more travel at night, for the terrain would not allow it. Hawthorne would maintain a course that would take them first to water and would then arc through the desert to Cairo Wells far to their west. It would not be an easy ride, but with luck he calculated that their odds were good. His chief concern was with the band of men dogging their trail. Could they continue to hold the lead they had on them? If not, a confrontation would definitely be to their disadvantage.

By noon, Malverne was exhausted. His clothes were sweat-stained, his head sagging. Although he had proven to be a good traveller to this point, it was obvious that the heat was taking its toll on him. Furthermore, his wounded arm was no doubt a factor, limiting his mobility and causing periodic discomfort. Lane was in a similar posture, although never complaining and continuing to do her best in moving at the pace set by Hawthorne.

By late afternoon, they stopped for their first full rest of the day. Hawthorne located a ravine whose overhanging walls afforded some welcome shade. Lane and Malverne dropped onto the sand as soon as they climbed out of their saddles. The horses were well lathered. Hawthorne gave them what water he could spare from the canteens, knowing that it was a mere pittance of what they required. Lane and Malverne also drank, but sparingly according to Hawthorne's directions.

"It's an inferno," Malverne announced, his face flushed and haggard. "I can't believe it could be this hot."

"Be thankful we found some shade," Hawthorne said. "There isn't that much to go around."

Malverne removed his Stetson and fanned himself

as he leaned against the wall of the ravine. "Are you sure there's no other way to go?"

"I'm afraid not."

Lane took a final sip from her canteen. Her blouse was wet, her hair straight. She seemed to be in a better frame of mind than she was on the previous night. She even managed a smile as Hawthorne sat beside her.

"I was in the desert once—five or six years ago. It was like a nightmare, a frightening nightmare. This is almost as bad."

"The desert can be like any other place. It can be cruel and unforgiving, but it has a beauty of its own, and it can be rewarding if you respect it," Hawthorne said, taking a sip of water and swirling it around in his mouth before swallowing it. "Look over there, for example, at the mariposa," he indicated, pointing at the rocky slope behind them. "You wonder how anything so beautiful can survive in this climate, but it does, and it flourishes."

"Yes, it is pretty."

"Sometimes I ask myself why objects of value like gold and silver are found in such forbidding, out-of-the-way places like the desert. Maybe it's because man was meant to sweat and strain and suffer in order to obtain them. That's one reason why they bring such a high price."

"I never thought of it quite that way," Lane mused.

"There's one thing for sure—if a man crosses the desert, he ought to have a good reason."

"It seems like another world, a place left to burn

itself out. I can't imagine anyone being able to exist here for any length of time."

"People can and do exist here. Some by choice, some out of necessity. The Apaches have learned to accept the desert life. They've adapted well."

Lane eyed him closely. "You seem to know quite a bit about it."

Hawthorne nodded as his eyes drifted across the sandy flats. "We should eat something." He broke out the jerky from his saddlebags and handed pieces to Lane and Malverne.

"I'm not hungry—only thirsty," Malverne announced.

"Try to eat it anyway. It will give you some strength."

Malverne nodded, bit off a small piece, and chewed it slowly while he closed his eyes.

Lane took some as well, reluctantly.

Hawthorne enjoyed a sizeable chunk as he stretched out his legs and relished the shade.

Thirty minutes later, Hawthorne urged them to mount up. Hawthorne switched to the spare horse, which was a bit fresher, having carried no one since they had started their trek.

For the next several hours, they moved steadily, through dunes dotted with cholla and catclaw, past jagged buttes and rock slides. They edged their way around lava beds, black and unearthly looking as though from a more primitive world. They made reasonable time and covered a respectable distance, but Hawthorne knew that neither Lane nor Malverne could go on much longer. Selecting a spot near a cluster of boulders, he called a halt to the day's travel. There were still two hours of daylight left, and he would have preferred to have pressed on, knowing that the men on their trail would not stop. However, he also appreciated that it would serve no purpose to be saddled with two exhausted, perhaps even sick people on his hands.

They made camp, rested, and ate. Except for a little coffee and some jerky, they finished the last of the food. There was little water remaining. There would be enough for a cup of coffee for each of them in the morning and a little left over for the horses. They would have to have water by nightfall of the next day.

Jed Hoskins dismounted his mare and bent over to examine her left foreleg. He had gradually fallen further and further behind Mace Gorman's lead until he was more than a hundred yards in the rear. Finally, Gorman and the others halted their march and rode back to determine what Hoskins's problem was.

"What is it, Hoskins? What's wrong?" Gorman asked.

"Stone bruise, I'd say. She's a strugglin'," Hoskins replied as he ran his hand up and down the animal's leg.

"You ain't likely to find any spares out here," Truman announced as he and the others formed a semi-circle around Hoskins.

"That's for sure," Burr Denton put in.

"You'll have to go back," Gorman directed. "Ridin' double will only slow us down."

"I can't make it back on foot."

Gorman scratched the stubble on his chin. "You're right. Talbot, you and Connors go back the way we came. The pair of you can take turns ridin' double with Hoskins here. You can always pick up one of the horses we ran off from the old man's spread."

Talbot and Connors, a pair of nondescript gunslingers who were comfortable following orders, did not argue, for they found no particular pleasure in continuing blindly into the desert anyway.

"Truman, Denton, and I will keep pushin' until we run down Malverne and that marshal."

"Right," Talbot said.

Gorman eyed the three carefully. "Oh, and before you go, leave your canteens with us. We'll likely need 'em more than you will where we're goin'."

Truman and Denton glanced at each other.

"How's that again?" Connors asked.

"You can get water back near the old man's spread," Gorman added.

"Yeah, if we make it back to the old man's spread," Connors returned.

"You shouldn't have any trouble."

"With two of us ridin' double and with no water at all?" Talbot added.

Gorman leaned forward in his saddle, resting his massive right forearm over the horn. "You know where you're headed. We don't. We're just trailin' that lawman. It could be a long time before we find any water at all."

"Yeah, well, I got a feelin' that that lawman knows exactly where he's goin', and I don't think he'd be fool enough to strike out blindly into the desert without knowin' where the next water hole is," Talbot said.

"Maybe, maybe not. Either way, where you're goin' is certain. Where we're goin' isn't."

"You don't ask a man to give up his canteen in the desert," Hoskins threw in.

Gorman eyed the three of them coldly. "The last I recall, I was the one runnin' this outfit, and nobody's told me different. Now, time's a-wastin'. I'm not askin' you to surrender those canteens—I'm tellin'."

For a frozen moment, no one spoke. Hoskins's hand drifted toward his holster but hesitated several inches before it got there. He glanced up at Talbot and Connors, whose eyes shifted back and forth between him and Gorman. The three of them quickly assessed the situation, figuring their odds. Each knew that Gorman, as fast as he was, could not take all three of them, but more than likely two of them would be left to die in the sand. After a long pause, they decided they did not like their chances. Talbot was the first to remove the canteen from his saddle and toss it to Gorman. Connors followed suit. Hoskins, more reluctant to yield his water, loosened his canteen and tossed it defiantly on the ground. He climbed up behind Talbot, stared sourly at Gorman, and the three of them rode off.

"Get that canteen, Truman. You and Denton share

it," Gorman ordered as he affixed the other two canteens to his saddle horn.

Truman did as he was told.

As Gorman watched the three men disappear behind some boulders, he grinned. "I always figured that twenty-thousand split three ways was better than six." He spun his horse and returned to the trail.

Truman and Denton stared at each other nervously as they fell in behind him.

At camp that night, Gorman, Truman, and Denton discussed their position. Gorman was stretched out on his bedroll, his hands clasped behind his head. "We're gainin' on 'em, that's for sure. They can't be movin' all that fast—a bookkeeper and a woman. They must be well tuckered out by now. That marshal can't travel any faster than the slowest one of them. I figure we can close in on 'em by dusk tomorrow."

"That's about as long as the horses are goin' to hold out, unless we find water," Truman announced.

"Do you think Talbot was right . . . I mean about this marshal knowin' where to find water?" Denton asked as he tossed another stick on the fire.

"I don't know. If he does, we can sure enough benefit from it. If he doesn't, he won't be able to ride many more miles. Either way, we've got him," Gorman replied as he pulled his hat down over his eyes and rolled over on his side.

After a few minutes, Denton leaned closer to Truman and whispered, "Either way, something's got to give by tomorrow."

Truman nodded. "I've been thinkin' about another point."

"What's that?"

"That $20,000. I'm wonderin' if it's goin' to be split up at all."

Denton rubbed his hand across his chin and spat out a thin stream of tobacco juice.

Hawthorne lay flat on his belly on a layer of rock atop a mesa. He looked through his spyglass at their back trail for a good many miles. A small cloud of dust distinguished itself from the surrounding terrain and translated to him that their lead on Gorman had been reduced to less than three hours. He made some mental calculations, collapsed the instrument, and descended to his horse. He mounted and met up with Malverne and Lane, who were in their saddles waiting.

"We're doing fine," he announced, hoping to exude a touch of optimism in his voice.

"They're still on our trail, aren't they?" Malverne asked, his face twitching in the glare of the sun.

"They're still there."

"We can't outrun them. There's no way we can make it to Cairo Wells before them," Malverne said with resignation.

"Not likely."

"Then what?"

"We'll have to outmaneuver them."

"That's Mace Gorman out there—Mr. McCargo's

chief henchman. Whatever else he may be, he's no fool."

"Yet we do have one advantage over him. We know where we're going."

Malverne seemed unconvinced by Hawthorne's cool assessment.

"He also has to be running short on water. That's a problem that has to concern him."

"As near as I can tell, that's our problem, too," Malverne returned.

"If we push hard, we should reach water by late afternoon."

"Will the horses make it?" Lane asked.

"They should. We'll keep alternating with the spare mount. They're tired and thirsty, too, but they should get us there."

The day's journey seemed longer and harder than the previous day's. If possible, the heat seemed greater. Lane was nodding in the saddle, and Malverne was flagging. Hawthorne was forced to stop and rest his small caravan more than he considered it wise to do. By early afternoon, he drained the final beads of water from the canteens onto his spare bandanna. He let the horses chew on the dampened cloth, affording them what little comfort he could.

It was later than Hawthorne had expected when he, Lane, and Malverne made a slight descent into a dry wash, the wash for which he had been searching. It led them on a serpentine route into a deep ravine that was peppered with mesquite and an occasional smattering of ocotillo. Here, beneath a rocky outcropping that offered welcome shade, Hawthorne called the others to a halt. Lane and Malverne could barely climb down from their saddles. They half-sat, half-fell onto the ground in the shadow of the overhang.

Hawthorne paced up and down the ravine, pausing occasionally to examine the sand at his feet. At one place near some shattered rocks, he knelt down and ran his hand through the sand. It was hot to the touch. He abandoned the spot and moved up the ravine a few yards, pausing near some catclaw, where he again studied the ground. Here, the sand was characterized by a slightly different grain and a scattering of fine scree. Hawthorne pulled the gloves from his belt and slipped them on. He knelt down and started to brush away the surface sand. For several minutes he occupied himself in this fashion, removing the sand until he had a bowl shaped depression a foot or so deep. He glanced around, spotted a flat stone the size of his hand, and retrieved it. Using the stone, he began to dig more deeply, clearing away the sand in larger and larger handfuls. After a time, he found himself breathing hard, more drained than he had realized. He sat down on the sand and rested.

Lane and Malverne were watching him through half-opened eyelids. There was deep concern on their faces as they waited and hoped for positive results.

Hawthorne did not realize how dry his mouth was. There was a gritty film on his teeth. What he wanted more than anything was to rinse his mouth and wash his face. In a few minutes, he resumed digging, using the stone again to deepen and broaden the hole. His strokes with the stone, however, grew shorter; the handfuls of sand that he removed became smaller. Again, he sat, catching his breath, studying the hole. It offered nothing but a darker shade of sand.

One of the horses nickered softly. Hawthorne climbed to his feet, straightened his back, and half-walked, half-tumbled into the shade, where he sat down heavily next to Malverne.

"The water . . . is it here?" Malverne asked in a voice that was barely above a whisper.

"It's here. I may have to dig another hole, but it's here . . . in this ravine."

"I don't see it."

"Water in the desert seems to have a mind of its own. Sometimes it acts as though it doesn't want to be found. You have to be patient and work at locating it."

Malverne rubbed his arm and closed his eyes.

Hawthorne glanced at Lane, who managed to smile at him through parched lips. He closed his eyes, deciding to allow himself a moment to rest before starting to dig again.

One of the horses nickered again, arousing Hawthorne, who had trailed off to sleep without realizing it. He sat up and focused on Malverne and Lane, who were both dozing. He forced himself to his knees, then his feet, and walked along the ravine once more. When he reached the hole he had dug, he saw a damp spot in the bottom the size of a silver dollar. The sight of it seemed to rejuvenate him, and he got down on his hands and knees and resumed his digging. This time he was fortunate to see quicker results as moisture began to seep through the sand and the damp spot grew larger. Soon, grains of sand began to swirl in a small puddle. As he dug, the puddle expanded until it became the size of a tea cup and then a dinner plate. Hawthorne removed his glove, dipped his hand into the liquid pool and held it to his lips. It was wet and soothing, and although he swallowed grains of sand with each sip he took, it was one of the best drinks of water he had ever had. He removed his bandanna, immersed it in the gathering pool, and wiped his face with it. It seemed to refresh him.

Hawthorne picked a canteen from the saddle of the nearest horse and carried it to the pool. He held it under the water, watching air escape in the form of tiny bubbles as he patiently filled the container to capacity. When he had accomplished this, he made his way to Lane, removed her hat, and sprinkled water over her face. She opened her eyes and looked up at him. He then held the canteen to her lips and let her swallow. The water revived her as she clutched the canteen and drank heavily. Hawthorne checked her, allowing her to recover slowly before taking too much. He then allotted her another sip before moving to Malverne and dousing him with water as well. Malverne's eyes opened, and Hawthorne handed the canteen to him. Malverne swallowed greedily at first, but when Hawthorne placed his hand on the canteen, Malverne nodded his understanding and began a series of sips to allow his body to absorb the water more gradually.

Soon, the three of them had washed and restored themselves. After the canteens were filled and the horses were watered, Hawthorne brought out the last strips of jerky, and they put some solid food in their stomachs.

Hawthorne then contemplated his next move. He calculated that they had an hour before Gorman arrived. With such a minimal start, he concluded that they would soon be overtaken in the open desert. He knew that Gorman needed water, and this was the only water for twenty miles. Sooner or later, Gorman would have to enter the ravine. A quick assessment of the terrain gave Hawthorne another option. From the top of the overhang, he could control the ravine. Any riders who attempted to enter would be fully exposed. Even if Gorman's gunhands chose to circle and enter the ravine from the opposite direction, he would still have the upper hand.

Hawthorne decided that the best place for Malverne and Lane would be atop the overhang with him. The horses he would have to secure somewhere in the ravine. He pulled his Winchester from its scabbard and started up the near side of the ravine. A quick reconnoiter to establish exact positions would be in order.

The top of the overhang was fairly flat, with a few small rocks and some mesquite. The protection, as far as it went, was not the best, but in any fight, it was always to one's advantage to take the high ground. He scanned the horizon to the east and saw a cloud of dust which he knew must be Gorman. It was more distinct now and moving in his direction. In an hour, perhaps less, they would have company.

His train of thought was broken as a red-tailed hawk raced past him, screeching discordantly as it nearly missed his head. A minute later, he heard a coyote howl somewhere off in the distance. Something was different. Something was wrong.

He knelt on one knee, clutching his Winchester loosely as he tried to reason out what it was that his senses were foreshadowing. Then, it came, not quickly but gradually. It started with a speck of sand that tickled his cheek. Then a grain caught the corner of his eye. He had to remove it with the tip of his finger. Next, a series of needles pricked the back of his neck, causing him to turn. That was when he saw it—far to the west, but moving toward him like a great billowing curtain. It rolled and pitched and skipped like an ocean mad with rage.

Sandstorm.

It was then that Hawthorne realized that they were trapped, wedged in between Gorman on one side and a storm of sand on the other. It was only a question of which one would reach them first.

Chapter Eleven

Hawthorne made up his mind. He descended into the ravine, returned the Winchester to its scabbard, and removed his lasso.

"What is it?" Lane asked, fear gripping her face.

"Sandstorm."

Malverne got to his feet and began to look around nervously. "We need to find cover."

"No. We're better off using the storm to our advantage. It will cover our tracks, and Gorman won't be able to follow us."

"But how can we travel in a sandstorm? We won't be able to see anything," Malverne countered.

"It won't be easy, but it can be done," Hawthorne said as he aligned the horses side by side, dallied the lasso around his saddle horn, and lashed the other mounts together in similar fashion. "Malverne, you

123

take the first horse. I'll ride the third, with the spare on my left. Lane, you mount up between us."

By this time, the wind had picked up, fanning the sand in the ravine, stinging and pricking with each successive gust. The ocotillo began to bend and twist in the air currents. The horses whinnied nervously.

Hawthorne loosened the bedrolls and tossed a pair of blankets to Lane and Malverne. "Use these for cover. Put them over your heads if you have to. You won't have to worry about where we're going. I'll see to that. Just make certain that you stay in the saddle. At all costs, stay in the saddle."

Lane and Malverne did as directed, holding on to their reins and clutching their saddle horns as well. Malverne had a difficult time with his arm in a sling, but he managed nevertheless.

Hawthorne wrapped his bandanna around the lower half of his face. He put on his coat and gloves and turned up his collar. He pulled his Stetson down low over his eyes and mounted. He urged his horse forward, and the others moved in tandem.

Slowly, they made their way out of the ravine, ascending a pebble-strewn slope for several yards before it graduated to level ground. From here on, the terrain was reasonably flat and unobstructed, but it also offered little protection against the pelting grains of desert sand.

Hawthorne maintained a slow but steady pace, keeping his head low so that his Stetson protected him against the searing blast. At times the air was so thick with sand he could not see ten feet in front of him.

He resorted to looking up only occasionally, to make certain that Lane and Malverne were still beside him and to maintain a westerly course.

The horses were uneasy, skittish, but they endured the rebellion of sorts that the desert hurled at them. They followed the pace Hawthorne set for them and plodded along. At one point, the trio rounded a tall finger rock that seemed to provide them with temporary shelter against the wailing wind. Hawthorne was tempted to remain here for a time, but he thought it best to push on for a while, and so he did.

The darkness cast over the land by the storm soon blended with the night as Hawthorne led the weary group into a narrow channel created by a pair of low ridges that flirted with each other but never quite touched. Here, he dismounted and loosened the lasso from the horses. He took the bridle of Lane's horse and led her into a gentle depression, the floor of which consisted of rock splinters and soft sand. Here, Hawthorne helped Lane dismount, and Malverne followed suit. Hawthorne picketed the horses and led the way past a twisted spine of rock to a small cave a few yards ahead. It was here that they spent the night, huddled around a meager fire that Hawthorne constructed mainly from some tumbleweed that had attached itself to a crevice in the rocks.

Malverne was spent. He fell asleep almost as soon as his head hit his blanket.

Lane sat close to Hawthorne, tired and edgy. Exposure to the storm had unnerved her.

"You know," she said, "a few days ago I was in

Uncle Cal's kitchen fixing dinner. Everything seemed to be going well for me for a time, following my pa's death, that is. Now, here I am, hiding in a cave in the desert, running from men I don't even know. It's all a little confusing."

Hawthorne nodded. "I'm sorry it had to be like this. If it's any comfort to you, it should all be over one way or another in a few days."

"It isn't. It's been like a bad dream. I can still see Uncle Cal lying there on the floor dying," she said, as her head drooped forward.

He put his arm around her and pulled her toward him, cradling her gently.

She looked up at him and smiled.

"You've been wonderful to me, Marshal, risking your life to protect Mr. Malverne and me."

"My friends call me Trace. I'd like you to call me that."

She laid her head against his chest, placed her hand on his arm, and closed her eyes. For the first time in a long while, she felt secure.

Max McCargo, his foot on the edge of his bunk, his hand wrapped around one of the bars of his jail cell window, stared out at the dirt street of Grand City. Hardly a city, Grand City was actually a town—his town, a town he had controlled for better than ten years. Somehow, it all looked different from a dingy cell. His perspective had changed.

He did not want to admit it, but deep inside he was becoming convinced that his way of life was being threatened by a growing segment of the populace that was increasingly concerned with law and order. For years his power had commanded enough influence and fear to obtain whatever it was that he wanted. Now, he found himself enmeshed in a legal wrangle that threatened not only his freedom but his very life. He had been responsible for the deaths and sufferings of many men over the years. It had been part of his nature, the way he had found easiest and fastest to rise to the top. Land, position, women—what he had wanted he had taken, and he never looked back.

However, confined to a cell, and with more time on his hands than he ever had, he began to reminisce about some of his acquisitions and conquests. He looked back on the many twists and turns that his life had taken, and after considerable reflection, he concluded that he wanted even more than he had. He wanted more of everything—particularly money, for money was power, and power was a weapon that no man could take lightly.

He turned away from the window, slumped onto the edge of the bunk, and began to assess his present predicament with the calculating eye of one involved in a high-stakes business transaction. Although he had heard nothing from Mace Gorman for several days, he was not concerned, for the gunman had never let him down. Because of Gorman's involvement, he felt confident that Malverne would never reach Grand City. Yet there were subtle indications that his stranglehold was getting weaker.

Myra, for example, had turned her back on him. She

was the first and only woman who had had the nerve. Before, it had always been he who turned away when he tired of a woman. Myra's actions could, of course, be explained away by her personality. She was different from every woman he had known—stronger, more intelligent. Most of his women had simply been passing fancies, temporary diversions who had sought him out. He rarely had to pursue a woman. They always found him; they were free with their attentions and their charms, and he never hesitated in taking full advantage of them. What particularly galled him in this instance, however, was that Myra had run off with Blake. Not only had a woman never turned away from him; no woman had ever given him up for another man.

Blake was McCargo's second concern. He was outraged to discover that his lawyer, whom he had manipulated for years, had been working behind his back, feeding information about him to the governor. Blake, though weak, was in his own way an intelligent, capable individual. It disturbed him to see Blake fleeing, like a rat deserting a sinking ship. He had ordered Blake's murder—following an interrogation—and Myra's return, but he had not yet heard from Brill Cotton. That troubled him. Surely, the pair could not have eluded Cotton, but if he had been successful, why had word not yet gotten back to him?

One of the deputies entered the lockup. McCargo glanced up as the man broke his concentration.

"Supper, Mr. McCargo," the lawman announced as he slipped a tray through the bars.

"Thanks, Grover."

The man named Grover nodded. He was about forty, of medium build, and clean-shaven. He wore a vest that advertised his deputy's star. He ran errands and did favors of a minor nature for McCargo from time to time. He was corruptible to a point, but McCargo knew that he and the other lawmen were under too close a scrutiny to be able to cross any serious borders. Besides, he knew the sheriff and the other deputies to be honest men. If there were a weak link in those lawmen around him, it was Grover. It could not do any harm to push him a little, just to see how far he would be willing to go.

"I got you a beefsteak from Ma Sweeney's," Grover said. "I know how you hate the restaurant's cooking." His facial expression was such that he was seeking McCargo's approval.

McCargo nodded. "Any messages or telegrams for me?"

"No, sir, nothing."

"Brill Cotton hasn't returned yet?" he asked, as he lifted the cloth napkin from the tray.

"No, sir, Mr. McCargo."

"Let me know as soon as he does."

"I'll do that."

McCargo cut a small piece of meat, eyed it critically, and then put it in his mouth. He chewed for a moment, nodded his approval, and then took a sip of coffee.

Grover seemed relieved.

"You're a good man, Grover. I appreciate these little things that you do for me."

"I try."

"Tell me, just how long have you been a peace officer?"

"Four years."

"You have a family?"

"Yes, sir. A wife and two boys."

"It must be . . . difficult surviving on your salary."

"The wife takes in washing. We get by."

McCargo smiled. "What is it they pay you—twenty, thirty a month?"

"Twenty-five."

"That isn't much for an honest man."

Grover shrugged.

McCargo took a bite of bread, wiped his hands, reached into his pocket and pulled out a fifty-dollar bill, which he slipped between the bars.

The muscles in Grover's jaw twitched as he eyed the money.

"Go ahead. You earned it by me. Take it."

Grover's hand moved hesitantly toward the bars. He paused, shot a nervous glance toward the door to see if anyone was watching, turned, and took the money.

"An honest man shouldn't have to struggle," McCargo stated, regarding Grover narrowly.

Grover returned his stare.

"Remember to let me know the minute Brill Cotton returns."

"I'll be sure to do that," Grover replied, nodding his head submissively as he backed out of the room.

McCargo smiled to himself as he picked up his knife and fork and cut his steak.

Chapter Twelve

Lane stirred slightly as Hawthorne removed her head from his shoulder and gently repositioned her on her blanket. Malverne still slept soundly as Hawthorne stepped past him, through the entrance of the cave. The sand on the floor of the cave and at the mouth had been swept into neat drifts that followed no apparent rhyme or reason as they filled tiny crevices and niches usually sought by insects and lizards. He checked the horses and found them exactly as he had left them, whinnying softly as he approached. One of them nuzzled him as he rubbed its ears.

He removed the spyglass from his saddlebag, retraced his steps from the previous night through the rock channel, and sought a point of high ground. The top of one of the rock spines served his purpose, and he searched out surface footholds as he climbed until he had easily scaled the craggy face. From here, he used the glass to track the desert floor. He began in the east, the direction from which they had come. He steadied the spyglass as he maneuvered it slowly until he had completed a 360-degree arc. The panorama offered a view of cactus, rocks, sand, a few buttes, and some distant mesas, but no life. Gorman, if he was still on their trail, was nowhere to be seen. At least, they had reestablished their lead.

As Hawthorne made a second sweep with the glass, he contemplated the terrain with a practical eye. The sky was all but clear, the sun was blazing, and the desert showed little change from the onslaught of the previous day. Harsh, uncompromising, and solitary, it changed very little, yet it changed every day. Just as each wave that struck a beach was different from the next, each sand dune cast a different pattern from one day to the next. The wind drew pictures in the sand, made blemishes on the rocks, and toyed with the plants. To an observant person, or to one who knew the land well, the desert could create more images than one could ever imagine.

Malverne was still asleep when Hawthorne returned to the mouth of the cave. Hawthorne nudged him and then moved to Lane, who was just beginning to stir. He roused her gently.

Lane sat up, her eyes still heavy with sleep as she ran her hand through her tousled hair. She smiled as she saw Hawthorne looking at her.

"Good morning, Marshal, I mean, Trace."

"Good morning, Lane," he returned, admiring her

as he began to roll up his blanket. He could not believe how good she looked so early in the morning.

"I must look a mess," she said self-consciously, assessing her blouse and brushing sand from her arms.

"I'd say you look pretty fine," Hawthorne returned as he strolled past her toward the horses.

She watched him as he walked by, smiled to herself, and then climbed to her feet.

Malverne rolled his blanket and carried it to his horse. Hawthorne took it and secured it for him.

"Any sign of Gorman?"

"None."

Malverne breathed a sigh of relief. "Do you think he could've found the water hole in all that sand?"

Hawthorne considered the question. "I don't know, but if he didn't, he won't last the day. There isn't any other water for close to twenty miles."

"You seem to know your way around this desert pretty well," Malverne said.

"I've spent some time here," Hawthorne replied, as he checked the cinch on the nearest horse.

"I don't know why anyone would want to."

"Sometimes people aren't given a choice."

Malverne stared at him, puzzled by his cryptic reply.

Sensing his confusion, Hawthorne followed with, "After all, we're here, aren't we?"

Malverne raised his eyebrows and nodded.

In a few minutes, Lane emerged from the cave.

Hawthorne handled her blanket and helped her to mount one of the horses.

"I know you're both hungry. So am I. We should have food and additional water by noon or so."

"I can make it," Lane said, smiling.

"Malverne?"

"Like you said, sometimes you aren't given a choice," Malverne added.

The three of them left the channel and rode on, pressing ahead at the pace Hawthorne set for them.

It was past midday when Hawthorne, Malverne, and Lane rounded a sandy slope adorned with primrose and cholla and entered a canyon, the floor of which twisted in the shape of a "C" before ending in a rocky cliff. Several adobe structures stood out on the canyon floor, solitary and morose in appearance. There were corrals, outhouses, a windmill, and a well.

The trio paused for a moment at the mouth of the canyon as Hawthorne surveyed the scene before them.

Lane and Malverne exchanged glances with one another, surprised at what they saw.

"Who lives here?" Lane asked.

"No one now," Hawthorne answered. "It was a small settlement, abandoned long ago."

"I've never heard of any settlement like this in the desert," Malverne stated.

"No, I imagine not too many people know of its existence even today."

"It's so remote—almost hidden," Lane offered.

"Yes, that was its purpose." Hawthorne tugged at his reins, steering his horse into the canyon, and the others followed.

At the nearest corral, Hawthorne dismounted. He opened the gate and led his horse and the spare inside. As he began to remove the rigging, he pointed to the nearest structure.

"Inside there you'll find some airtights, some cookware, and a stove. I'll tend to the horses and fetch some water if you two will get some food started."

Lane and Malverne dismounted and stepped toward the adobe building. Malverne turned the handle of the door and found it unlocked. They entered a fair-sized room with a fireplace at the south end with a pile of sticks stacked inside. There was little furniture—a wooden table, some chairs, and a cabinet. Shelves were neatly lined with some tins. There were earthenware dishes and cups, some pots, and a lantern. There was an order about the room, except that a thick layer of dust blanketed everything.

Malverne conducted an inspection of a pair of rooms that ran off of a short hallway. He found some beds and some simple furniture, all dust-laden and seemingly forgotten.

Lane read the labels on the tins. She found some peaches, beans, and beef. There was also a small sack of coffee. She located a knife and went to work opening each container.

In a while, Hawthorne entered with a bucket of water. He helped Lane wash off the table, dishes, and cups while Malverne started a fire in the stove.

Soon, they sat down to eat. Lane truly enjoyed the peaches, especially the sweet juice in the tin. Malverne and Hawthorne preferred the hot beef and beans. After half an hour they had all eaten their fill, leaned back in their chairs, and quietly discussed their newly found luxury.

"I do believe that's the best meal I've ever had in my life," Malverne announced, patting his stomach.

"Thanks a lot. What about my stew and cornbread? It wasn't so long ago that you praised that so highly."

Malverne cleared his throat. "Beggin' your pardon, miss."

Hawthorne smiled. "Either way, it's your cooking that's being appreciated."

Lane bowed her head with a flourish.

"How did you know about this place?" Malverne asked, glancing around the room.

"I come here from time to time, use it as a camp when I'm crossing the desert. I stock it with supplies when I can," Hawthorne explained.

"Did you know the people who lived here?" Lane asked.

"I did."

"What became of them?"

"Some died, others moved on. After a time, there was no reason for any of them to remain here," he said, a note of sadness in his voice.

"What did they do out here in the middle of nowhere?" Malverne inquired.

Hawthorne took a sip of coffee and stared at the

table before him. "Survived the best they could. They caught and broke wild horses, raised some sheep. They even did a little mining. There's a small copper deposit beyond the canyon walls. It didn't yield much, but it helped them along."

"There's something sad about this whole place," Lane said. "I feel lonely here, as though I'm at the end of the earth."

Hawthorne shrugged. "There were some happy times here. There were good feelings, and love and companionship despite the harshness of the land and the remoteness."

Lane eyed him closely, detecting something in his voice that she could not fathom.

Hawthorne drained the last of the coffee from his cup, a faraway look in his eyes. Finally, his thoughts seemed to return to the present, and he pushed himself away from the table. "We're all tired. I thought we'd spend the rest of the day here as well as the night. We can get an early start in the morning and be in Cairo Wells the day after tomorrow."

Malverne and Lane seemed relieved by the words.

"Sounds good to me, I'm whipped," Malverne said, fatigue written on his face.

"Me too. I can't imagine going another mile," Lane added.

Hawthorne nodded. "Good, then it's settled." He climbed to his feet. "The horses need more water. I'll see to them."

"I could use some myself. Is there enough to wash?" Lane asked.

"There's always plenty of water here. In fact, there's an old metal tub in the last adobe structure. I'll be glad to fill it for you."

"Wonderful! Do you think I'd be able to wash my clothes?" Lane asked, looking at herself and wriggling her nose.

"Sure. I'll string a line for you behind the building. I should even have an extra shirt around here somewhere. You're welcome to it while your clothes dry. I'll give you a call when I have everything ready."

She beamed her thanks, the smile brightening her tanned face.

"Malverne. What do you need?"

"Right now, I'll settle for another cup of coffee. Then, one of those beds looks pretty good to me. I'll bet I could sleep for two days."

Hawthorne picked his Stetson off the back of his chair and walked outside.

Malverne poured himself more coffee while Lane began clearing the table.

Hawthorne made a slow walk to the well, where he filled a bucket and poured it into a trough next to the corral. He repeated this procedure several times until the trough was about half-filled. The horses shuffled over, stuck their heads through the corral poles, and began to drink.

There was a small outbuilding nearby. Hawthorne opened the door and removed a bag of feed. The horses were down on their weight following their trek through the desert, and they needed a bit of fattening. He watched them for a while as they enjoyed themselves before he filled another bucket with water and toted it to the last of the buildings. He rinsed out the tub for Lane and then filled it after a series of trips to the well. He hung a clothesline as he had promised and located a clean shirt, which he hung over the side of the tub. He then poured some water into a deep bowl, which she could use to wash her clothes. He placed a cake of soap and a clean towel next to it.

Lane was ecstatic when she saw what Hawthorne had done for her. She pushed him out of the room, closed the door, and immediately began to remove her clothes. As she eased into the tub, she found the well water cool and refreshing. She enjoyed it for several minutes as she rested her head on the rim of the tub and closed her eyes. Then, she took the cake of soap and started to scrub. It felt good to remove the sand and dried sweat. She could not remember a bath that she needed or enjoyed more.

There was still a full bucket of water beside the tub, and she used it to wash out the sandy grit from her hair. She was reluctant to leave the coolness of the water, but it had served its purpose in revitalizing her. Finally, she climbed out of the tub and slipped into the shirt Hawthorne had left for her. It was too big all over. The sleeves hung way below her fingertips, and the shirttail fell nearly to her knees. She laughed, as she could only imagine what she must have looked like, but she rolled up the sleeves and went to work at washing her clothes. The blouse, one of her favorites, would probably never return to its original appearance, but it was all she had left in the world. She did what she could and when she was done, she hung the blouse, the denims, and her undergarments outside to dry. Then, she returned to the adobe to do what she could with her hair.

Chapter Thirteen

Lane's clothes were still a bit damp when she put them on again. She decided to take a stroll to let the desert air finish the job. She walked further into the canyon, rounded some boulders, and came upon a path. She followed it for a short distance before it ended in an isolated hollow. What she saw here took her by surprise. There were three graves, covered by stones, marked by crosses. She approached them out of curiosity. There were no names to offer any identities, only desert poppies strewn across the stones. The white, wrinkled petals of the flowers seemed to offer a marked contrast between two worlds; one a sad and dusty past, the other offering brightness and hope. Lane stood by the graves for a long time, pondering. Someone had only recently placed the poppies on the stones. She concluded that it could only have been

Hawthorne. Who else even knew of this seemingly forgotten settlement in the middle of the desert?

The sun was losing its strength for another day when Lane returned to the main corral. Hawthorne was approaching from the direction of the well. He had shaved and washed and looked like a new man. She smiled at him, and he smiled back.

"You certainly look handsome this evening, Trace," she said, taking his arm.

"And you look fresher and prettier than you did the first day I saw you," he returned.

"You didn't tell me I looked pretty the first day you saw me," she countered.

"Didn't I? That's strange. I usually let a woman know just how pretty she is."

"And have you made the acquaintance of many pretty women?"

"Oh, dozens, but not many as pretty as you . . . in the desert, that is."

She glanced up at him, realized that he was teasing her, and laughed.

He laughed back, and they walked together back to the adobe house.

Malverne was standing next to the stove. He turned when they entered and eyed them curiously.

"Well, two more handsome people than you I've not seen in a while," he said.

"It's amazing what a little bit of soap and water will do," Lane replied.

"I had it in mind to make myself another cup of

coffee," Malverne announced, "before I go back to bed again."

"I'll make it," Lane offered.

Malverne sat at the table as Lane filled the coffee-pot.

Hawthorne removed his gun belt and hung it on a wall peg. He picked up the lantern, lit it, and placed it on the table. Then, he sat next to Malverne. Hawthorne watched Lane, appreciating the results of her bath. He liked the way her hair fell around her shoulders, and he liked the clean, fresh way she smelled when she was near him. He wondered if she ever sang around the house or if she enjoyed quiet walks. He caught himself thinking about Lane in a way he had never thought about a woman. In the past, there had been romances, but he had never allowed himself to get too close. Now, however, his mission was nearly over. In a matter of days, his life would change. He might even give up his badge and his itinerant way of life . . . if there were a good enough reason.

His thoughts led him to consider Malverne as well, the small sad man who had travelled so far with him to give testimony. Malverne, who had been personally wronged by Max McCargo, had expressed little hope in even reaching their destination. He had undergone a change, however, and had shown more courage than Hawthorne thought likely during their experiences.

"What will you do, Malverne, when this is all over?"

Malverne shrugged his shoulders. "Provided that I survive to give testimony, you mean?"

Hawthorne nodded.

"I haven't given it much thought. Go back East, I guess. There are plenty of businesses that can use a bookkeeper, and I am good at what I do."

"Do you have friends back East?" Lane asked.

"Not really. I don't have any friends anywhere."

"You're a good man, Mr. Malverne. I'm sure you'll do just fine wherever you go," she said.

Malverne smiled. "Thanks, miss, but I'm not the type to make friends. I live in a world of cramped offices, of pencils and paper, bills and receipts. It isn't very exciting, and consequently, I'm not a very exciting man."

"What you're doing takes grit. I don't know many men, even men who are good with a gun, who would be willing to buck the odds against McCargo the way you are," Hawthorne stated.

"That's kind of amusing. Ever since I agreed to give testimony, I've felt like a dead man. I've been running scared ever since."

"But you went ahead anyway, and you're here, only a few days away from Cairo Wells and the trial."

Malverne nodded, forcing a jittery smile. "Yes, and the more I think about it, the more I've come to believe that I have a chance, a good chance of stopping Mr. McCargo and maybe of starting over again." He shook his head as if in disgust. "You know, after all he's done, after all the people he's hurt, I still call him 'mister'."

Hawthorne and Lane exchanged glances as they considered Malverne's words. Both of them felt sympathy for him as he sat at the table, small and lonely, but hopeful.

The quiet interior of the room was suddenly shattered as the door crashed open. Lane dropped a tin cup, which clattered on the floor. Hawthorne and Malverne turned in shocked surprise and half-rose from their chairs. All eyes focused on the doorway, where Mace Gorman stood, his huge shape nearly filling the threshold, the wooden door dangling loosely on broken hinges. Gorman's eyes were narrow, his jaw set, his clothes sweat-stained and dusty. He stood motionless, like a statue, his Colts drawn and pointed.

Malverne gasped as he fell back into his chair, his face ashen with fear.

Lane's hands moved quickly to her face as she stood in terror, frozen to the floor.

Hawthorne's eyes ran to his gun belt, a good six feet away on a peg. He knew it would be a fool's move to try for it, and he slowly sat back down in his chair, cursing within for permitting himself to relax for even a moment.

For a long time, Gorman said nothing. He merely stood in the doorway, his eyes taking in every detail of the room. Finally, his lips curled cruelly as he took a step forward and holstered the Colt in his left hand.

"Well, well . . . it's nice to see all of you, happy and comfortable in this cozy little hideaway. I have to admit, you led me on quite a chase." He leveled the barrel of his gun on Hawthorne. "You'd be the lawman, Hawthorne."

"That's right," Hawthorne replied, resting his arm on the table.

"I've heard tell of you." His eyes assessed Hawthorne carefully. "You know this desert like a rattler."

"I'm surprised to see that you found us. I didn't expect you to locate the last water hole, especially not in that sandstorm."

"I didn't," Gorman said, grinning. "In fact, if it wasn't for the good-natured side of a couple of my compadres, I wouldn't have made it here at all. You see, they decided that I should have their water. It's too bad that they won't be around to share in my good fortune," he said, laughing to himself.

"Even so, it's a hundred-to-one against your picking up our trail again after the storm," Hawthorne added.

"Well, you see, that's where I got to thinkin'. Some of my boys were talkin' about how smart you were and how you knew exactly where you were headed. I knew you weren't bound for Grand City, so I figured your only other likely destination had to be Benton Mesa or Cairo Wells. They both lie in pretty much the same direction. I decided to ride that way and, lo and behold, I stumbled across your trail again. My horse gave out six or seven miles back, but I managed to make it the rest of the way on foot. By the way, the water from your well tasted mighty good. I'm feelin' strong again, real strong," Gorman said, grinning again.

"You worked hard to get here. Your loyalty to McCargo is impressive," Hawthorne said.

"It ain't pure loyalty. Mr. McCargo put a bounty on Malverne here. He's worth $20,000 on the hoof."

Malverne's eyes widened.

"That's a lot of money," Hawthorne said.

"Enough to do me just fine."

"But chicken feed to a man like Max McCargo."

"I ain't greedy. Never have been."

Hawthorne glanced across the table at Malverne and then looked at Gorman again. "Just how do you expect to collect it? McCargo won't be able to pay it. He'll be found guilty and executed."

"Not without Malverne, he won't, and Malverne won't be testifyin', will you?" He turned his attention to Malverne, who looked away, disheartened.

Hawthorne shifted uneasily in his chair.

"Enough talk. Miss, get me some coffee and grub. I ain't eaten in a while," Gorman ordered.

Lane looked at Hawthorne, fear in her eyes.

Hawthorne nodded.

She moved, awkwardly at first, her hand trembling as she reached for a bowl.

"You, lawman . . . on the floor over there, your back against the wall," Gorman said, leveling his gun at Hawthorne.

Hawthorne did as he was told, backing away from the table until he reached the wall. Slowly, he sat down on the floor, drawing his knees up to his chin.

Gorman sat down at the table and placed his Colt in front of him within easy reach.

Malverne started to rise, but Gorman clamped his huge hand on the bookkeeper's shoulder. "You stay right where you are. I paid hell to find you, and you're not gettin' out of arm's reach until I decide exactly what to do with you."

Malverne did as ordered, his hand moving nervously up and down the sling of his wounded arm.

Lane placed some beef and coffee in front of Gorman and then quickly retreated away from him.

Gorman hastily went to work on the meal. He smiled his approval as he ate and drank heartily. When he was done, he tapped his cup on the table, and Lane refilled it. When he was satisfied, Gorman wiped his mouth on his shirtsleeve and sucked his teeth. He leaned back in his chair and folded his hands across his stomach as he contemplated first Lane, and then Malverne.

"You know, I've been wonderin' . . . Mr. McCargo might just be inclined to pay me a tad more if I brought you in and let him do the job himself. I imagine he'd take great pleasure in slicin' you up, bleedin' you a little at a time until the life oozes out of you. Yes, sir, he just might show his gratitude if I handed you to him on a silver platter. What do you think, little man?"

Malverne looked away, his jaw twitching uncontrollably as he considered Gorman's remarks.

"What's the matter? Cat got your tongue?"

He lashed a backhand across Malverne's wounded arm.

Malverne flinched in pain but did not speak.

"Still pinin' over that gal of yours, the one that did herself in? She wasn't anything special from what I heard, and I got the word straight from Mr. McCargo himself."

Gorman's last comment struck a nerve, and Malverne turned to face him.

Gorman leaned back in his chair again, folded his hands over his stomach, and flashed a taunting smile at Malverne.

Malverne suddenly appeared to be ready to explode.

Hawthorne had never seen him angry and worried that the timid bookkeeper might do something foolish. Hawthorne placed his hands palm downward on the floor, ready to spring to his feet if the opportunity arose.

Malverne's eyes bored into Gorman, his anger now overriding his fear of the big man. He rubbed his sore arm, his hand moving in and out of the sling. Suddenly, he reached out and knocked Gorman's Colt off the table and onto the floor. He then reared back and struck Gorman across the face. The blow, ineffectual in itself, nevertheless took Gorman by surprise. Infuriated by so unexpected a move, Gorman punched Malverne, who toppled over his chair and fell hard to the floor. Grimacing in pain, Malverne lay where he had fallen.

It was only a slight distraction, but it was all that Hawthorne needed. In an instant, he pushed himself off the floor and lunged toward the table. Gorman's left hand moved like a snake toward the Colt in his holster, bringing it out in the blink of an eye. Hawthorne gripped the table legs and flipped the table over onto Gorman, knocking him out of his chair and to the floor. He threw his weight against the table, pinning Gorman's gun hand under the edge. Gorman's Colt discharged, but with his hand pinned as it was, the bullet aimlessly struck a wall.

Hawthorne kicked the Colt from Gorman's hand, but before he could make a move for it, Gorman pushed up the table, with Hawthorne still on top of it, and overturned it, sending Hawthorne reeling backward until he struck the wall behind him.

Gorman got to his feet with remarkable quickness for such a big man, and he stepped toward Hawthorne, his fists clenched and his arms in front of him in a fighter's stance.

Hawthorne regained his balance and met him halfway. Wasting no time, Gorman swung a sweeping right cross. Hawthorne stepped under it and fired two jabs into Gorman's ribs, which felt like iron against his fists. Gorman swung again, wildly, and again Hawthorne eluded the blow, but Gorman's third effort hit home, striking Hawthorne squarely in the middle of his face. Hawthorne's head snapped back and again he was driven against the wall. Blood began to trickle down his lips and chin, and he knew that his nose was broken. He shook his head to rid it of the cobwebs and came out in a crouch, bobbing and weaving, avoiding Gorman's melon–sized fists, which sliced through the air like windmill blades in a cyclone. Hawthorne continued to deliver short, sharp jabs to Gorman's midsection, but the big man showed no signs of slowing his attack.

Gorman feigned a right and then caught Hawthorne

on the cheekbone with a punishing left. Hawthorne was seeing double as he circled just out of Gorman's reach. Gorman continued to move in to press his advantage. Overconfident, he telegraphed his left-right combination, and Hawthorne made him pay. Hawthorne arm-blocked both punches, stepped inside, and delivered an elbow to Gorman's throat. Gorman's eyes widened as he searched for breath, clawing at his windpipe with both hands. This left his stomach unprotected, and Hawthorne took advantage of it by delivering a series of blows that could not help but take effect. Gorman bent over, dropping his head, and Hawthorne brought up his knee, connecting solidly with Gorman's jaw with enough force to bend him over backward and send him sprawling onto the floor.

Heaving for breath, Hawthorne remained planted where he was in the middle of the room, bent over, not knowing whether Gorman would rise again.

Ten seconds later, Gorman began to rise. Slowly, he climbed to his knees, panting, pushing himself off the floor with shaking hands.

Bleeding, his shirt torn, Hawthorne looked on, wondering if he had any strength left if Gorman were to mount another attack.

Gorman put one foot on the floor and sneered at Hawthorne. "I'm gonna finish you now, lawdog."

Hawthorne took a deep gulp of air and stepped forward. Cupping both hands together, he swung at Gorman in a downward arc with everything he had, only hoping that he had enough coordination left to connect with the big man. Fists met jaw, Hawthorne felt his knuckles sting, and Gorman went down, his head coming to rest on the floor, his mouth open, his arms hanging awkwardly at his sides.

Hawthorne stumbled across the room, where he righted a chair and collapsed into it.

Malverne was still on the floor, leaning on his good arm. With some effort, he sat up and looked at Gorman.

Lane began to cry. She approached Hawthorne tentatively at first and then rushed to his side and threw her arms around him.

For a long moment, no one spoke. Hawthorne leaned forward, holding his head in his hands.

Lane removed Hawthorne's bandanna, dipped it in water, and began to dab the cuts on his face.

Hawthorne winced, and when she touched his nose with the bandanna, he could feel the pain. He took her hand in his and held it to his nose, telling her without words how much it hurt. He had no words at the moment.

Lane placed her other hand on his shoulder and braced him tenderly.

A scraping sound caused Hawthorne to turn.

Lane looked up and screamed.

Gorman had come to and crawled over to one of his Colts on the floor. He picked it up and cocked it.

Hawthorne looked to his gun belt, still out of reach.

A sudden shot rang out, loud within the confines of the adobe walls. Gorman's head jerked backward, a small hole appearing in his forehead before blood oozed out. His Colt dropped to the floor as his head pitched forward.

Hawthorne and Lane looked at Malverne, who was still sitting on the floor, holding a derringer in his hand.

"I had it in my sling," he said, half talking to them and half to himself. "I don't know why. I never knew I could ever use it. Gorman took it away from me once, humiliating me. His mistake was in giving it back."

Chapter Fourteen

Hawthorne wrapped Gorman's body in a blanket and placed it in one of the outbuildings. He walked back to the house, shut and secured the broken door as best he could, and sat down stiffly at the table. His face was bruised, and he looked weary.

"I'll help you bury him in the morning if you'd like, Marshal," Malverne offered.

"No, I don't want him buried in the canyon. We can bury him on the way to Cairo Wells."

Lane sat down beside Hawthorne, her eyes locked onto his. "This was your home, wasn't it?"

Hawthorne nodded.

"Those graves at the far end of the canyon—they're people you knew."

"My mother and father . . . and my uncle," he said, a distant memory reflected in his eyes.

Malverne sat down beside them and rested his good arm on the table.

"What exactly happened here, Trace? Why were you and your folks living out here in the middle of nowhere?" Lane asked.

Hawthorne took a deep breath and let it out slowly between swollen lips. "It's a story that goes back a long way. It's about bitterness and fear and revenge . . . and any way that you look at it, it can't have a happy ending."

He glanced up to see Lane and Malverne looking at him, deeply curious yet at the same time not wanting to hurt him by dredging up the past.

"I'm thirsty, Lane. Is there any coffee left?"

Lane nodded, filled a cup, and set it before him.

He took a sip and then placed it on the table in front of him, staring at the brew. He considered them carefully for a long moment before he finally nodded his head and said, "It's probably best that the story is told once and for all. Besides, in a matter of days, the final page will be turned." He took another sip and leaned forward, placing his arms on the table and cradling the cup in his hands. "I first came to this canyon when I was ten years old. Altogether, I spent eight years of my life here and in the desert surrounding us. This is where I grew up. This is the land I know.

"It started for my family shortly after the War ended. My father and uncle fought on the Union side, the 27th Indiana under Colonel Colgrave. There were honors for some, but for them there was tragedy, at a place called Chancellorsville. My uncle lost his arm, and my father received a chest wound that severely damaged his lung. It gave him coughing fits. The doctor told him he needed a warmer, drier climate. It was for that reason that my family sold our farm and packed everything we could carry into a pair of covered wagons and headed west. There were thousands of families moving west at the time. Some were Oregon-bound for the timber and the rich farm soil. Others had their eye on the gold fields of California. My father was just searching for a small plot of land where he could start a farm or a ranch and maybe get rid of the cough that plagued him. My uncle . . . was just searching for a place to start over and sometimes, I thought, for a place to hide. He never seemed to be able to get over the fact that he would be a cripple for the rest of his life.

"We met up with a wagon train in Springfield, rode with another forty or fifty families through most of Missouri until we branched off for a more southwesterly route. The days turned into weeks and the weeks into months. We were near the end of our journey when my mother came down with the fever. She was weary from the endless miles of travel, the heat, the dust, the insects, all the hardships of trail life. She was suddenly overcome with it all and fell into a terrible sickness.

"We did what we could for her to make her as comfortable as possible, but nothing worked. Finally, we came to a small town called Copper Creek. It wasn't on any map. It doesn't even exist anymore—just a ghost town on the fringe of the desert. There couldn't have been many residents. When my father asked if there was a town doctor, they immediately became suspicious. They were scared, scared of something I had never heard of when I was ten. It was called cholera. They had had an outbreak of the sickness not long before we arrived. I never saw such people—nervous, edgy.

"There was a doctor. He came out of his office, and he seemed to be willing to treat my mother, but the others wouldn't let him go near her. They said that he was the only doctor in better than fifty miles, and they didn't want to risk losing him to the sickness. The sheriff was the worst of the lot. He grabbed the bridle of our wagon's lead horse and refused to allow my father to advance any further.

"My father pleaded with them, begged them, offered them money—everything he had if they would only allow the doctor to help my mother. They refused. I was afraid. My father was desperate . . . about to reach for his rifle when the sheriff drew his gun. He ordered us to leave his town at once. My father and uncle had no choice. The sheriff and several other men with rifles rode behind us for miles to make certain that we didn't turn back. When we were well out of sight of the town, they forced us to ride on into the desert, where we didn't know what lay ahead. It was almost the same as murder.

"When night came, the townsmen were far behind us. My father and uncle stopped our wagons and made camp. My mother was worse. There didn't seem to be anything that we could do. My father and uncle talked it over. My uncle agreed to stay with my mother and me while my father returned to town to make another try for the doctor. He figured to at least get some medicine for my mother if he couldn't bring the doctor himself. It was a dangerous and desperate move, but my father was at his wits' end. He kissed my mother and drew me close to him. He looked at me in a way that I had never seen him look at me before. He saddled a horse and slipped out of camp. I was afraid I would never see him again.

"I couldn't sleep that night. I was too worried about my mother and father. I sat with my mother and talked to her, trying to comfort her as best I could. To this day, I don't think I've ever been more frightened in my life than I was that night.

"It was nearly morning when my father rode back into camp. He was alone and disappointed and with less heart in him than I had ever seen before. The story that he related to my uncle and me shocked us both. It was late when he had returned to Copper Creek. He managed to sneak into town without being seen. The townspeople appeared to return to their normal routines. He located the doctor's house and waited in some brush nearby, making certain that there was no one around. When he felt confident that no one was watching the back of the house, he entered through an unlocked door. He stood in the darkness for some time, listening, straining to hear any sound. Hearing nothing, he made his way through the house until he saw a crack of light under a door off the main hallway. He still heard nothing, but he was cautious, nonetheless.

He pushed open the door slightly and saw a man in a chair. His back was to my father; he was slumped over a desk. There was an oil lamp on a table on the far side of the room. It offered little light, leaving most of the room in heavy shadows.

"My father entered and called to the man at the desk. When there was no response, my father stepped closer. That's when he saw a knife buried in the man's back. It was the town doctor. My father was too shocked to move. Then, he sensed the presence of another in the room. He turned toward the light in time to see a big man emerge from the shadows, a gun in his hand. My father managed to knock the gun away. The two of them struggled, turning over furniture, banging into one of the walls. Finally, my father was able to gain the upper hand. He struck the other man, dropping him to the floor, then ran from the room. Before my father was out of the house, however, he could hear the man shouting, calling out 'murderer.' My father thought the shouting would rouse the entire town. He found his horse, and as he rode out, he saw lights appearing in some of the windows.

"During his scuffle in the doctor's office, my father had torn something from the other man's clothes. He had held it tightly in his hand and, while he escaped, had crammed it into his pocket. He had forgotten all about it until he returned to our camp. As he was finishing his story, he removed the article from his pocket and held it in his palm near the light of our campfire. It was a sheriff's star."

Lane gasped when she heard Hawthorne's last remark.

Malverne, entranced by Hawthorne's narrative, leaned closer. "Do you mean to say that the town sheriff killed the doctor and tried to pin it on your father?"

"Yes."

"But why?"

"We didn't know at the time, but we learned some six months later that the sheriff married the doctor's widow."

Lane and Malverne remained silent for some time, digesting what Hawthorne had told them. Finally, Lane asked, "And your mother? What became of her?"

Hawthorne frowned. "My father feared that the townsmen would pursue us because he had left an easy trail to follow across the desert sand. We broke camp at first light and pushed hard across the wasteland. We were well into the desert and running low on water when an old Mexican sheepherder named Romero came out of nowhere and found us. He led us to water, here in this canyon. He lived here, on and off, as he traveled through the desert. One of these adobe huts was his. He helped us to care for my mother. We all did the best we could, but by then it was too late. She was very weak—from everything. It wasn't cholera, just trail fever. We buried her here in the canyon, and with her, we buried a part of my father as well. From that day on, his spirit was broken; his will was gone.

"A month or so later, my father decided to return to Copper Creek to set matters straight. My uncle thought it was a bad idea and so did I, but my uncle decided that if anyone returned, it should be him. That's when Romero intervened. He made occasional trips to Copper Creek to buy supplies and sell his sheep. He offered to visit the town and to learn as much as he could of the incident before any of us returned. My father and uncle thought that made good sense. They would remain behind and tend Romero's herd.

"When the sheepherder returned, nearly a week later, we were all shocked by the news that he brought. The doctor had indeed been murdered, and not only my father but my uncle as well had been charged with the crime. The townspeople didn't know their names, but they issued wanted posters bearing the likenesses and descriptions of my father and uncle. Romero brought one with him.

"Both my father and uncle were outraged when they saw it. They picked up their rifles and started to saddle their horses, but again the wise Romero calmed them. He made them realize that they would be heavily out-numbered and that the townsmen, having lost their doctor, wouldn't be in any frame of mind to take the word of two strangers over the word of their own sher-iff. My father and uncle were still upset until Romero reminded them of their responsibilities to me. He told them that I would be left alone if they did not return. Hearing this seemed to change their minds. Romero explained that there was safety here in the canyon for all of us because nobody ventured this far into the desert except the Indians, and they rarely came near the canyon, perhaps because they realized that Romero posed no threat to them. My father and uncle agreed to stay where they were, to bide their time . . . and stay they did.

"Romero proved to be not only a good friend to us, but a wise man as well. He helped us to build these adobe houses. He taught us the ways of the desert, helping us learn how to survive and even prosper. He became another uncle to me, allowing me to travel with him far from the canyon. He taught me the land—the plants, the animals, the water holes. In time, I became a confident traveler in a land that most men shunned and feared. He was a good old man. I imagine he must have been sixty or more when he first came upon us, but he never seemed to change through all the years I knew him. His hair and beard were always white, and he always wore a straw hat and a serape. My father, uncle, and I helped Romero with his flock. As time went by, we developed our own small enterprise. We became mustangers. I learned how to ride and rope and break horses. We built corrals and pens. Romero became our frontman. Through him, we were able to sell our stock and make enough money for supplies and even extras.

As the months turned into years, my father and uncle eventually ventured to some of the small towns on the far side of the desert, risking their freedom to conduct business, to see things, to be around people again. In my father's case, I don't think it made that much difference, for I knew he would never leave the canyon permanently. I knew he was bound there because of my mother, for he visited her grave every day. My uncle, as well, appeared reluctant to leave. Maimed as he was, he never seemed totally comfortable around people.

They both worried about me, for they knew that I couldn't live in the desert forever. My father secured books for me and helped me with my studies. He knew that in time it would be best for me to leave and be among others my own age. For myself I didn't mind. I enjoyed the solitude of the land, and I wanted to be with my father and uncle, the only kin I had left. I knew they were innocent fugitives who would never be able to clear their names; I knew they would always be looking over their shoulders, but I was content to live the life they did.

"As the years passed, my father's cough grew worse. It had subsided for a while, but it never really stopped completely. As it worsened, he began to lose weight. We urged him to see a doctor, but he refused. Six years after we entered the canyon, he passed away. A year and a half later, my uncle died. Romero helped me to bury both of them.

"I stayed on in the canyon for a while, but I had no one; I knew no one except Romero. He helped me to mold my plans. My father and I always talked about what I wanted to do when I got older. I heard him tell me many times that this part of the country needed honest lawmen. I suppose his words influenced me more than I ever realized. I decided to become a lawman, partly because I wanted to help and protect people, but in all honesty, I also had revenge in mind. I remembered the sheriff of Copper Creek and how he had used his position to destroy my family. I didn't want to gun him down in the street like a hired assassin. If I did, I would've become an outlaw myself. I would've lived the rest of my life as my father and uncle had. Instead, I wanted to use my authority in some way to bring him to justice.

"Romero traveled with me across the desert to a town where he knew the sheriff. He somehow got him to take me on as his deputy. It was menial work at first—sweeping the floor, making coffee, checking door locks at night. In time, however, my duties expanded. I was eighteen, green, and I made mistakes, but I learned. I learned the law, and I lived by it and respected it. I also became proficient with a gun, a skill that kept me alive during encounters with men who respected only lead. Five years later, the sheriff retired and I replaced him.

"Romero came to visit me from time to time, and whenever I had the chance, I would return to the canyon to see him. He always put desert flowers on the graves for me. Then, there came a time when the good old man passed on. He was as valuable a friend as anyone I ever had.

"Some time later, on business, I traveled through the town of Copper Creek. I didn't know how I would handle myself or what I would do if I encountered the sheriff. I never got to find out. The town was deserted—boarded up, abandoned for other claims. The mine had paid out, and there was nothing left of the people who had forced us into the desert or the sheriff who had framed my father and uncle for the crime he had committed. He could've been dead for all I knew. I asked questions as I traveled, but no one seemed to know anything about the town or the sheriff. It was almost as though the town had never existed and the incident had never taken place.

"The years passed, and I became a marshal. I was based in a town called Spencer, although my duties required me to travel extensively, mostly through the southern part of the state. You can imagine my surprise when one day, as I was passing through one of the smaller communities on my circuit, I heard the sheriff's name. He was no longer a lawman. He was wealthy, powerful. In time I was reading about him in newspapers, but there were sinister rumors about his activities. For years there were rumors. Then came accusations, but there was never any evidence. Witnesses were paid off or mysteriously disappeared. I began to take a professional as well as a personal interest. He was protected by many. Although I was never able to touch him, at times I was able to thwart his plans and help some of the small people from being trampled by his machine.

"There came a time when his offenses could no longer go unchallenged. The governor himself took a hand. Events brought the two of us together, just as events have brought me here to this canyon once again."

As Hawthorne concluded his narrative, he looked up and saw Lane's and Malverne's eyes affixed on him. They had listened to every word he had spoken and were still digesting the incidents he had detailed.

Malverne spoke first. "But, Marshal, you're talking about Mr. McCargo."

Hawthorne nodded. He pulled a small leather pouch from his pants pocket. Placing it on the table, he opened it and removed a sheriff's star. "This is the star that my father tore from the sheriff of Copper Creek the night he was framed for murder. Read the inscription on the back."

Malverne reached for the star and turned it over. His eyes widened as he read, TO SHERIFF MAX McCARGO FROM THE CITIZENS OF COPPER CREEK.

Chapter Fifteen

The sun was high in a sky that had only a handful of stationary white clouds. A lazy hawk circled overhead, occasionally dipping in search of a meal.

Lane took a long swallow from her canteen as she regarded Hawthorne, who sat quietly in his saddle, studying the terrain ahead. In addition to all of his other qualities, she was most impressed with his patience. He was the kind of man who waited until he was certain and then went ahead. She liked that in a man.

Hawthorne finally turned in his saddle and looked at Lane and Malverne. Pointing ahead, he said, "There, just beyond that rise, is Cairo Wells. Two more miles and we're home free."

Malverne smiled. "To be honest, I didn't think we'd get half this far."

"There were times when I wasn't so sure myself," Hawthorne replied.

"And now the trial. You did your job. You kept me alive. You delivered me. Now, it's my turn to tell the story of Max McCargo."

Hawthorne considered Malverne closely. "You know, in all the miles we've traveled together, I don't think I've ever heard you call him anything but mister."

Malverne shook his head. "You know, you're probably right. I guess maybe I'm just not so afraid of him anymore."

Hawthorne smiled. He nudged his horse and led the way to Cairo Wells.

A mile or so from town they picked up a trail. Half a mile more they saw a pair of riders kicking up some dust as they slowly approached.

Hawthorne held up his hand for the others to stop. He halted his horse in the middle of the trail and waited, his eyes fixed on their new company. With his right hand, he loosened the thong on the hammer of his Colt.

As the horsemen drew closer, Malverne announced, "It's all right. They're lawmen. They're wearing badges."

The two men were similar in appearance, both wearing broad-brimmed Stetsons, dark coats, and, as Malverne observed, badges. They were both mustached, wore hand guns, and appeared trail-hard. One of them sat a little taller in the saddle and cradled a Winchester in his left arm. They stopped half a dozen feet from Hawthorne.

"Marshal," the one with the rifle said, half in the form of a greeting.

Hawthorne nodded.

They looked over Hawthorne and then carefully checked Malverne and Lane.

"My name's Costigan. This here's Hicks. We're special deputies, sworn in by the governor himself. We've got orders to escort you and your witness into Cairo Wells."

"Is the governor expecting trouble?" Hawthorne asked.

"Can't rightly say. We're just followin' orders."

"Uh huh. Well, then I suggest that you follow these. Drop that rifle and lose those sidearms. Turn your horses around and ride in front of us," Hawthorne ordered.

The two men exchanged startled glances and then looked back at Hawthorne.

"Marshal, we—"

"I guess you boys didn't hear me the first time. You either drop those weapons or use them."

Neither man spoke. Costigan's face began to twitch just below his left eye. For a moment, everyone sat frozen in his saddle. Then, Costigan suddenly swung his rifle barrel around.

Hawthorne drew and fired his Colt. The shot was loud. His bullet struck Costigan in the shoulder, knocking him out of his saddle.

Hicks's hand was on the handle of his gun when Hawthorne turned his Colt on him and cocked it.

"I can put two rounds in your heart before you can clear leather," Hawthorne stated flatly.

It took very little time for Hicks to consider Hawthorne's words. Slowly, he raised his right hand and unbuckled his gun belt with his left, letting it drop to the ground.

"How many more of you are there in town?" Hawthorne asked.

"None."

"How did you know about Cairo Wells?"

"Costigan there got a telegram from somebody tellin' us you'd be here."

"Who?"

"I don't know, and that's on the level. I just follow orders."

"How long have you been in town?"

"Since this mornin'. We rode hard through the night to get here."

"Why'd you cover this trail?"

"His idea," he replied, nodding toward Costigan.

Hawthorne elevated the barrel of his Colt. "I'm going to ask you again. How many more of you are there in town?" There was a hard edge in his voice.

"Like I said, none. There's only the two of us."

Hawthorne's eyes turned cold. "I see you're not wearing a bandanna. Here, take mine. Tie it around your right thigh," he said, as he loosened his bandanna and tossed it to Hicks.

Malverne and Lane exchanged glances.

Hicks had a puzzled expression on his face as he caught the cloth. "Just what are you aimin' to do?"

"I don't like your answer. There are three ways into this town. The stage carrying McCargo will be coming from the north. That road will be swarming with deputies. That leaves the south road and this trail. You wouldn't cover one and not the other, not with two men. That means somebody else is watching the south road."

Hicks's face suddenly reddened, and he licked his lips.

"Wounded men have told me that the two most painful places to be shot are in the stomach and the knee. Being a lawman, I won't gut-shoot you, but I'll shatter your kneecap sure enough."

"Now, hold on, Marshal. All right. It's as you said. There were four of us who rode in. The others are coverin' the south road."

"Who are they?"

"Randall and Larson."

"Stone Randall and Gar Larson?"

"That's right."

"What did you do with the sheriff?"

"He's alive. We took him and his deputy by surprise when we rode in early this mornin'. We got 'em hog-tied in an outbuilding behind the jailhouse."

Hawthorne shifted in his saddle as he digested the gunman's story. "All right, help him up. Get him in his saddle. The two of you will be riding in ahead of us. If anybody tries anything, you'll be the first to get it. Understand?"

Hicks nodded and did as he was told.

Malverne brought his horse up alongside Hawthorne's. "How did you know? I mean that they weren't lawmen?"

"The governor and I had our own arrangement. My job was to deliver you from doorstep to doorstep. He knew that I worked alone. There were to be no contacts in between unless they were my own. There were too many who couldn't be trusted. I knew the governor wouldn't send any deputies unless I requested them, and I never did."

Malverne nodded. "Then that means that if these men are here, in Cairo Wells—"

"That McCargo already knows about the change of venue. He wasn't supposed to find out until today. He won't be transported until tomorrow. That would've given us time to get you into town and placed under heavy guard. Someone leaked the information."

"Someone in the governor's office?"

"I don't think so. Not this time. By now the governor's sure to have taken care of that. No, I think it's more likely that the leak came from Grand City."

"In either case, we're too late if McCargo's men are already here," Malverne said, a defeated expression on his face.

"Maybe not. If Hicks is telling the truth, he and the others weren't notified until yesterday, and they just arrived. McCargo may not have had time to get any more of his men here yet. We still have a chance of getting you into town if there are only two more men on the south road. We'll take it slow and easy. Either way, we don't have much choice."

Hawthorne was familiar with the layout of Cairo Wells. He chose to avoid the main street, opting instead for a meandering path through a pair of alleys that served to bypass the usual traffic they might have encountered. He moved tentatively, alert to any unusual activity, ready for any unexpected movement that might signal an assault. He directed Costigan and Hicks down a side street that led to the rear of the sheriff's office while Lane and Malverne trailed a short distance behind. He ordered the gunmen to dismount and then followed suit, drawing his Colt as he approached the back door.

Hicks helped Costigan maneuver up a trio of wooden steps. Pointing to a shed next to a six-foot stockade fence, he said, "You'll find the sheriff and deputy in there. They're not hurt."

Hawthorne nodded, glanced up and down the street, and motioned for the gunmen to enter the jail.

"You'd better wait here," Hawthorne said to Lane and Malverne. "Dismount and stand between your horses. Be alert."

"Right," Malverne replied as he pulled his horse alongside Lane's and helped her dismount.

Hawthorne found the sheriff's office empty. He put Costigan and Hicks in separate cells and quickly returned the way he had come. As Hicks had indicated, he found Sheriff Tom Barlow and his deputy Mac Campbell in the shed. They were both conscious but bound tightly and gagged. Neither was in a hospitable mood.

Five minutes later, the sheriff, deputy, Lane, Malverne, and Hawthorne were all in Barlow's office. Hawthorne had made all the introductions.

"You're a sight for sore eyes, Trace," Barlow announced. He was fifty, tall, thin, clean-shaven, with watery blue eyes.

"What happened?" Hawthorne asked.

"They took us by surprise. We weren't expecting anything like this, at least not before McCargo showed up."

"The one in the far cell says there are two more on the south road."

"That makes four and that's right," Mac Campbell put in as he poured coffee all around. "Two of 'em came through the back door while that pair came through the front, bold as rattlers in a prairie dog hole."

"Where are your other deputies?"

"On the north road, workin' out security arrangements with Sheriff Landry's men out of Grand City. They should be back any time now."

"Good. I want two men on Malverne until he walks into that courtroom."

"You'll have 'em, Trace. By the way, what happened to him?" Barlow asked, nodding toward Costigan.

Hawthorne frowned. "He had a notion of using a Winchester on me. He'll need a doctor."

"And he'll have one, just as soon as Mac and me

settle a score with that pair on the south road," Barlow said as he removed a scatter gun from his rifle rack.

Campbell strapped on a holster and checked the cartridges in a .45 he picked up from the desk.

"In the meantime I'd like to get Malverne secured and find a hotel room for Lane," Hawthorne said.

"Sure thing, Trace." Turning to Lane, he said, "Miss Carter, you'll enjoy the hotel. The dinin' room has good food."

Lane took a close look at herself. "I'm hungry, but what I really need is a hot bath and a change of clothes."

"I'll have Miss Evans in the dress shop drop over and take a look at you. I'm sure she can rustle up a new outfit for you."

"Thanks, Sheriff," Lane said with a smile.

Barlow stepped over to his desk, opened a drawer, and pulled out a key, which he handed to Hawthorne. "For Malverne's special quarters," he said.

Ten minutes later, Hawthorne unlocked a small room within the courthouse itself. He ushered Malverne inside and made a close inspection. A cot, a chair, a table, a washbasin, and some foodstuffs had been allocated for Malverne's convenience in a room that was six-by-eight. A small window near the ceiling accessed the alley at the rear of the building for ventilation.

"Exactly where are we?" Malverne asked, glancing around him.

Hawthorne tapped on one of the walls. "You're

about two inches away from the judge's chambers and ten feet from the courtroom."

"Can't I stay in the hotel?"

"Not a chance. I won't risk losing you now to a sniper as you walk across a hundred feet of open ground between the hotel and the courthouse. You're here, and here you'll stay until you give testimony. Only a select number of people know about this room. It's been converted just for you."

Malverne removed his hat, hung it on a peg, and sat down heavily on the cot. "Well, after the trip we've just taken, including spending the night in a cave, I guess it isn't as bad as all that. Besides, I'll probably spend most of the time sleeping until the trial starts. I'm spent."

"There will be hot meals and anything you need. Nobody will enter but me. I have the only key. I'll put a man just outside the door in case you want something. Another man will be in the vicinity."

Hawthorne turned to leave.

"Marshal."

Hawthorne paused.

Malverne extended his hand. "Thanks for keeping me alive and for . . . for everything."

Hawthorne clasped Malverne's hand and shook it firmly. "Good luck, Malverne, with the trial and . . . with the rest of your life."

Two weeks later, Max McCargo's trial was over. He was convicted of a series of capital offenses and sentenced to hang. Two days before his execution was scheduled to take place, he requested that Trace Hawthorne visit him in his cell. Hawthorne agreed to see him.

McCargo was seated on his cot, leaning against the wall, his arms folded across his chest, his legs stretched out on his mattress. When he saw Hawthorne enter, his eyes narrowed and he stood up. For some time, neither man spoke. They just stood some six feet apart and stared at one another. Finally, McCargo stepped to the cell door and wrapped his hand around one of the bars.

"You'd be Hawthorne," he said.

Hawthorne nodded.

"I saw you in the back of the courtroom every day during the trial. You've been in my way for a long time, and for the life of me, I can't figure out why. I don't know you. I've never seen you before."

Hawthorne stood there silently, his eyes hard and unforgiving.

"Well, why don't you say something? Don't tell me it's your job or your respect for law and order. It has to go deeper than that to do what you've done to put my neck in a noose."

Hawthorne regarded him closely. McCargo had changed considerably from the first time Hawthorne had seen him, but the cold, lifeless eyes were the same, as was the cruelty that registered in his lips.

"Well, don't just stand there. Say something, Hawthorne!"

"You've seen me before. Think back . . . a long time

ago, Mr. McCargo, or should I call you . . . Sheriff McCargo?"

McCargo's eyes widened.

"Think back to a town called Copper Creek, a dark night, a doctor—a doctor that you murdered."

McCargo's jaw suddenly dropped, and his face seemed to shrivel. He started to speak but could only stammer. "You . . . no, you couldn't know about that. You're too young."

"The men you framed were my father and uncle. The sick woman you sent away was my mother."

"You . . . were that runt kid."

"That's right. I was that runt kid."

"I thought all of you died in the desert."

"In a sense, we did, thanks to you. You covered your tracks very well. You made certain that my family were fugitives from the law, fair game to be shot on sight if they survived and if they ever attempted to tell the truth about you." Hawthorne pulled McCargo's sheriff's star from his pocket and held it up in front of McCargo's face. "I can't tell you how many times I've dreamed of pinning this over your heart and putting a bullet through it."

McCargo nodded, the full light of recognition slowly dawning in his eyes. "I've stepped on a lot of men during my life. I won't deny it, and I can't say that I'm sorry. It was the only way to get what I wanted, and I wanted it all. I wanted that doctor's wife back in Copper Creek. She ended up leaving me, you know." He grinned broadly. "You should've seen the expression on her face when I told her years later that

I was the one who killed her husband. She even tried to shoot me herself."

Hawthorne shook his head. "You're worse than something I'd step on in a pig sty."

McCargo's eyes narrowed.

"I only hope that this country never sees the likes of anything that resembles you again."

"Why you fifty-dollar-a-month lawdog. Nobody talks to Max McCargo like that! I've bought lawmen like you by the handful."

"Not like me, McCargo. My badge has never been for sale. You've bought men like yourself."

A sneer formed on McCargo's face as his hand tightened around the bar.

"I hope you have a short, quick drop to hell."

"Why, you—"

McCargo's hand suddenly snaked through the cell door, clutching for Hawthorne's throat, but Hawthorne caught his wrist and held it tightly in his left hand. In ten seconds, McCargo began to grimace, trying desperately to pull away, but Hawthorne held him until he winced with pain. Finally, Hawthorne released him. McCargo held his wrist with his other hand, rubbing it as he glared hatefully at Hawthorne. Without warning, he lurched through the bars again, this time reaching out with his left hand. Hawthorne sidestepped him and shot his fist through the bars, striking McCargo squarely in the mouth. The blow sent him spinning backward until he fell onto the cot and then toppled over to the floor where he lay shaken, a trickle of blood running down his lip and off his chin. It took half a minute for him to clear his head and focus his eyes again on Hawthorne.

"This is the way I'll always remember the great Maximilian McCargo . . . blood dribbling from his lip onto his starched white collar and silk vest, his dignity gone, sitting on his backside on the floor of a dirty jail cell in a small town." Hawthorne tossed McCargo's sheriff's star on the floor. "It's time you reclaimed your property. I've carried it long enough. Maybe they'll put it in your coffin with you."

Most of the patrons had completed their breakfast, and the restaurant was almost deserted. Hawthorne finished his third coffee. He glanced across the table and found Lane's eyes locked on him. She was wearing a pretty white dress with small red buttons and red swirls across the bodice. Her hair was combed to perfection, and her eyes were bigger and darker than he had realized.

"What will you do now, Trace, I mean now that your job in Cairo Wells is done?"

"I figured on returning to Spencer. Then, I think I'll give notice. I've worn a badge for a long time now. It's time I settled down, stayed in one place."

"Ranching?"

He nodded. "I've got some money saved. I have an option on some land. I thought I'd start a small spread, maybe raise a hundred head or so. It's not much, but it's a beginning."

"Sounds good," she said, with one of those smiles that set his heart to racing.

"It could be."

Lane looked out the window at the activity in the street. She started to say something but decided against it.

"And you? Will you be headed back East?"

"I imagine so. With Uncle Cal gone, I don't suppose I'd have any reason to stay."

Hawthorne found himself to be nervous, edgy. Did he have the right to ask her to spend her life with a wandering desert man like him?

"You're young and strong. The West needs women like you."

She considered him closely, realizing that he might not get much closer to a proposal without some urging. "A rancher needs a good wife . . . someone to cook and clean, and raise his children," she said.

They smiled at one another.

He suddenly realized just how pretty of a girl she was. He reached his hand across the table toward hers, and she took it. It was a small hand, almost delicate wrapped as it was in his fingers, but it was also strong in its own way.